S0-ANE-168

APR -- 2023

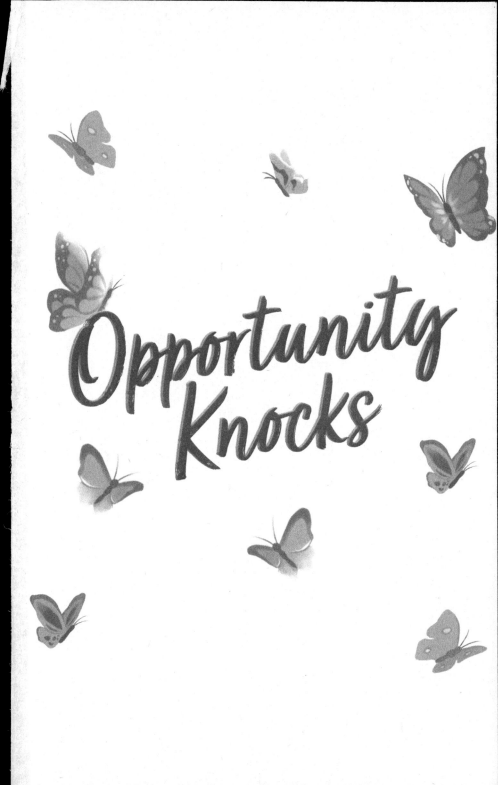

SARA FARIZAN

Opportunity Knocks

 SCHOLASTIC PRESS
NEW YORK

Copyright © 2023 by Sara Farizan

All rights reserved. Published by Scholastic Press, an imprint of Scholastic Inc., *Publishers since 1920*. SCHOLASTIC, SCHOLASTIC PRESS, and associated logos are trademarks and/or registered trademarks of Scholastic Inc.

The publisher does not have any control over and does not assume any responsibility for author or third-party websites or their content.

No part of this publication may be reproduced, stored in a retrieval system, or trans-mitted in any form or by any means, electronic, mechanical, photocopying, recording, or otherwise, without written permission of the publisher. For information regarding per-mission, write to Scholastic Inc., Attention: Permissions Department, 557 Broadway, New York, NY 10012.

This book is a work of fiction. Names, characters, places, and incidents are either the product of the author's imagination or are used fictitiously, and any resemblance to actual persons, living or dead, business establishments, events, or locales is entirely coincidental.

Library of Congress Cataloging-in-Publication Data available

ISBN 978-1-338-82707-1

10 9 8 7 6 5 4 3 2 1   23 24 25 26 27

First edition, February 2023

Printed in the U.S.A.   37

Book design by Omou Barry

For my cousin Rana, who makes me feel
lucky to share laughs with her

Chapter One

Lately it feels like everyone has found their *thing*. I guess I was absent the day I was supposed to do that.

I miss kindergarten. I was really good at being five. Was that my best year? I mean, is that when I reached my peak? Now that I'm in middle school, it seems to me that everyone has figured out who they're going to be and what they're going to be great at. I haven't found my *thing* yet, but whatever it is, I hope I find it soon.

I tried joining robotics club, but every time I got near a soldering iron . . . well, let's just say I'm glad the fire extinguisher was nearby.

I tried out for the school play, but I forgot my lines

during my audition. I was offered the role of a tree. But that would have meant I would be the only tree onstage— as everyone else who auditioned got a part with lines. I thought that wasn't the best use of my time. Chess club was a little too quiet. Debate club was a little too loud. I tried out for soccer because my best friend, Melanie Choi, is a star on the team, but it wasn't for me. There was a lot of running involved . . . while having to do other stuff at the same time as the running.

But there was one school activity that I knew everyone who wanted to participate in could. And that's where I find myself now.

"Lila?" Mr. Hernandez says from the front of the band room.

"Yes?" I ask. I glance at my fellow bandmates seated behind their instruments. It feels nice to be a part of a group, even if it is a small one.

"You're the big finish," Mr. Hernandez reminds me.

"Oh! Right. Sorry," I say. I do my part in band practice. I hit the triangle. Mr. Hernandez says I can work my way up to a more complicated instrument when I feel ready.

"Thank you. Please, don't forget your cue next time," he says warmly.

The other eight kids in band don't laugh because they aren't so hot at their instruments either. Well, except for Carolina. She's really good at piano, but she plays outside school at fancy recitals. She's very nice about it, but if I were as good at piano as she was, I'd play all the time and let everyone know it was me playing. *Did you hear that Chopin down the hall? The music that made your heart swell? Yeah, that was me! I know! I'm so good!*

"If there is a next time," Jimmy says under his breath. I think he's always in a gloomy mood because of what he plays. He sees himself as a drums guy, but his parents got him an oboe.

"What does that mean, if there's a next time?" Carolina asks.

Mr. Hernandez lets out a sigh. It's the kind of sigh teachers make when it's the end of the week before spring vacation and nobody pays attention in class anymore.

"I was holding off on letting everyone know until later in the semester," Mr. Hernandez says, "but band may be coming to an end."

"What?" Veronica on flute says. "What about our concert?"

"The concert will still happen," Mr. Hernandez says. "However, due to budget cuts and lack of interest, the school is considering dropping the music program next year."

Just when I was finally getting the hang of the triangle! I feel like my dings are really making an impact!

"Isn't there anything we can do?" I ask.

"We'll figure something out," Mr. Hernandez says, but he's making that face grown-ups make when they don't know what to do.

❦❦❦

My best friend, Melanie, runs up to me from the soccer field sideline. Her face is sweaty and her black hair is up in a ponytail with a white ribbon in it. I don't tell her, but I'm always envious she gets to wear it on game days with her teammates. I have black hair too, but I still haven't figured out how to *embrace my curls* like my mom says I will.

"Great game," I say.

"We lost," she says with a disappointed chuckle.

"Yeah, but you scored two goals!" If I ever scored a goal, I wouldn't be able to stop talking about it! "That's a big deal! Everyone was cheering."

She shrugs. "It takes a team to win," Melanie says. "I should have passed more." She's always hard on herself when it comes to sports. I wish I could say something that would change that for her. "We'll be ready next time. Thanks for coming."

"I wouldn't miss it," I say, and she smiles. We've been best friends since kindergarten. (As I said, my best year.) "You ready to walk home?"

She looks over her shoulder at her teammates. They're eating orange slices and joking around with one another.

"We're all going for pizza with Coach. Want to come? I bet you could!"

"Oh. No, that's okay," I say. I didn't play a tough game. Pizza is for the team. I'm not on any team. "I'll catch up with you tomorrow."

"Definitely," Melanie says, swooping in for a hug. "Sorry, I forgot I'm kind of sweaty." She laughs as she backs away.

"It's okay," I say. I didn't feel any sweat, but she did play a hard game, and I can see sweat on the bridge of her nose and on her temples.

"See you tomorrow!" she says and then jogs back to her teammates. One of the players gives Melanie a distinct handshake with fist bumps and snaps involved. I walk home alone, thinking about how Melanie and I don't have a secret handshake like that.

"Lila joon, you haven't touched your dinner," Mom says at our kitchen table.

"It's delicious . . . if I do say so myself," Dad adds. He always feels proud when he makes dolmeh. I put my fork into the grape leaf and bite into the rice so they don't worry. Despite my lack of appetite, it's still warm and tasty.

"Did something happen at school?" Mom asks. She can always tell when I'm upset. Mom tries to help, but sometimes she doesn't know the right thing to say. At least she tries, and she always gives me a kiss on my cheek when I'm feeling down.

"Mr. Hernandez says the school might be cutting band," I say.

"How can that be?" Mom asks.

"I bet it's because of the construction of the new gym," Dad says, shaking his head. "You know, it might not be a bad idea to try out for basketball next season." I play for fun with my dad and our family watches a lot of basketball on TV, but I don't know if I'm good enough to be on our school's team.

"I like band," I say. Which is partly true. I mean, I am happy to be there, but the group hasn't really warmed up to me yet. We don't have secret handshakes, like Melanie's soccer crew. But it feels like it's only a matter of time! I've wanted a *thing* to be a part of for so long. Now that I finally found one, it's being taken away.

"Of course you like band," my older sister, Parisa, says. "All you have to do is hit the triangle."

"Parisa, I don't care for your tone," Mom says.

"I'm sorry but the triangle isn't an instrument!" Parisa says, cutting up her food into tiny pieces. "It's a tool to let people know when meals are ready on a ranch. Why don't you try playing something cooler while you still can?"

That's easy for her to say. My sister is a sophomore in

high school. She gets lots of trophies for all the things she's involved in. And they aren't even participation trophies! She wins stuff all the time and I'm reminded of it in every room of the house. We're running out of space for Parisa's accomplishments. The other day, I found a volleyball trophy in the bathroom medicine cabinet. I didn't even know she played volleyball.

"I could see you rocking out with an electric guitar," Dad says to me with a gleam in his eye. He had that same gleam when Parisa told him she wanted to study premed at college. I don't know how she's already found the *thing* she wants to do for the rest of her life. Maybe when you're great at everything, it's easier to choose.

"I don't know if I'd be any good at it," I say. Then I shove a whole stuffed grape leaf in my mouth.

"You'll never know unless you try," Parisa says. "Do you think I would have won those concert tickets if I didn't call into the radio station?"

A year ago, my sister won backstage passes to Pop Fest 3000 and didn't take me. I'm still upset about that, but she never noticed.

"You got lucky," I say in between chews.

"Winners don't need luck," Parisa says, leaning forward in her chair. "Winners take a chance on themselves because they believe in themselves. Your trouble is you don't think like a winner."

"Life isn't all about *winning*," Mom says. "I think what your sister is trying to say is that if you like music, we'll help you figure out ways to keep the band going."

I don't know what *thinking like a winner* means, but maybe I could try to find a way to raise money to save the band. Then I could figure out what I'm meant to be great at.

Chapter Two

I had an epiphany before bedtime last night about where I could come up with some funding for my school. I thought it was a pretty solid plan when I entered the bank, but the way the man behind this desk looked at me when I told him I was his three o'clock appointment has me worrying I'm in a little over my head.

"What is it that I can assist you with, Ms. Moradi?" Mr. Stuart asks me. "A savings account perhaps?" We're sitting inside his cubicle, not one of the offices that have doors. He's white and looks like he can't be that much older than Parisa. His suit doesn't seem to fit him right, but he's made an effort with his pocket square. He's being polite, but I can tell he's trying to get rid of me as fast as he can. He keeps looking at the clock above my head.

"I was wondering if you could help me get a loan?" I ask. He blinks at me for a moment. I worry maybe he didn't hear me. "My school is going to cut the music program. I want to figure out a way to save it."

"I see," he says as he nods. "While I commend your efforts, what kind of collateral would you have to offer?"

I read about how to get a loan online, so I came prepared. Collateral means stuff that the bank can take if you don't have money to pay back the loan. I put my backpack on my knee and take out the items that I thought might help my cause.

"This is the crème de la crème of my comic book collection," I say as I pull out a fat stack of vintage comics. They're all in good condition and bagged and boarded. Mr. Stuart doesn't pick them up; he just glances down at them. "It mostly features a lot of *The Woodchuck Brigade.*"

"I'm sorry?"

I don't know if I can trust a man who doesn't recognize greatness when he sees it.

"*The Woodchuck Brigade.* They're a bunch of woodland creature supersleuths who morph into robots when they're called upon by the citizens of Munkerton to save the day. They had a cartoon show for three seasons. I felt it could have gone longer, but the writers kept recycling old story lines toward the end, which I think is what caused the ratings to tank." It was my favorite TV show when I was a kid. Parisa always thought it was kind of goofy. I figured if I could trade the comics in for the band, it would be a sign of maturity.

"Ms. Moradi, this is a lovely gesture and I'm sure your school appreciates it, but I think if a loan is something you would like to pursue, it would be better discussed with a parent or a teacher." Mr. Stuart looks over my head at the clock again.

"I haven't shown you my trading cards yet," I say as I dig into my backpack. I'm about to show him the good stuff.

"That won't be necessary," he says. He opens a drawer and slides a pamphlet across his desk to me. On it is a smiling guy who has just opened his own cupcake business. The title reads *Make Your Dream a Reality with a Loan from Providential Hills Bank*.

"Take this home. Talk it over with an adult and feel free to reach out to us again after you do," Mr. Stuart says. "Is there anything else I can assist you with?"

"So, does this mean I'm not getting the loan?"

"Not today, no," he says as he extends his hand to my comic books. I put them gently into my backpack along with the pamphlet. "Contact me once you can schedule a time with a guardian. My card is in the pamphlet. May I interest you in a lollipop?"

I nod. I might as well leave here with something. He motions to the mug with Dum Dums in it. I pick Cotton Candy flavor. He must think I'm a dumb dumb too for not having the kind of collateral the bank is looking for.

"I look forward to hearing from you," he says with a fake smile that lets me know he isn't. I want to get out of here. I bolt up from my chair and exit his cubicle. I feel someone bump into my shoulder from behind. I stumble a little but stay on my feet. I turn around and see an old white man walk past me. He turns his head, and I think he's going to apologize.

"What is a child doing here?!" the man bellows. "This is a place of business, not a day care center." He's bald, short, stocky, and looks like he's never smiled a day in his life. I want to yell at him that I'm in middle school and definitely don't need day care (though the toys the toddlers play with do look like fun sometimes), but he keeps walking and doesn't notice the CAUTION WET FLOOR sign in between the giant marble columns leading to the doors. He slips, and his legs are about to go into a split, when I see five bank employees rush over to make sure he doesn't fall.

He's bent forward and about to keel over, but two employees catch him and right him on his feet. They ask him if he's okay, if they can assist him with anything, and call him Mr. Mammonton. Everyone around him is super-duper nice. They seem kind of scared of him, so I guess he must be important. The man brushes them off and leaves the bank, and I can see him through the revolving glass door as he climbs into the back seat of a fancy car that a driver has opened for him. The bank employees whisper to one another as they watch his car leave. I take a step forward and my foot hits something. I look down and see a small wooden box.

Nobody pays me much attention when I pick it up to look at it. It's a plain, worn, old box. The only thing interesting about it is a deeply carved inscription on the side that reads: "A simple clue for you who holds the key, remember to unlock the door for opportunity." I peek inside the box to find a small, bronze, antique-looking key.

Mr. Stuart marches toward the front.

"Mr. Stuart," I call out to him. I'm about to tell him that somebody misplaced the box. But he doesn't hear me, or pretends he doesn't, and joins his fellow employees to talk about Mr. Mammonton.

I don't see a lost and found sign like at school. I'd like to give this to someone in charge, but everyone seems kind of too busy to notice me. I put the box in my backpack. I'll bring it back when I come visit the bank with Mom or Mr. Hernandez. Then hopefully someone will take me seriously.

Chapter Three

I didn't tell my parents about my trip to the bank. I was embarrassed and didn't want Parisa to find out that Mr. Stuart thought my comics were as silly as she did. I *try* to like the stuff that Parisa likes, but she makes every activity into a competition so then it's no fun anymore. I spent a lot of Saturday and Sunday looking up Mr. Mammonton on my computer, though. I found out he is very, very, *very* wealthy. He even had a new factory built right in town recently, though I don't know what they actually make there. He also seems to have a hobby of collecting artifacts from far-away countries and funding archaeological digs in places that he probably shouldn't. It seems more like he's stealing pieces of history that don't belong to him—they belong to the people whose history it is.

In all the photos of him, he always has a scowl. I've heard the expression *money doesn't buy happiness*, but maybe he's not spending it the right way.

I put the small box on my nightstand next to my bed so I won't forget to return it. Hopefully, when I do give it to the proper person at the bank, there might be some kind of reward. I could use the money to save the music program. Then Mr. Hernandez, Carolina, Jimmy, Veronica, and everyone else in band would thank me and we'd feel like a real team. One that goes for pizza together after a great recital. Anyway, whomever the wooden box belongs to, I can't be sure they're missing it an awful lot. It's kind of a banged-up, forgettable box—except for the little poem carved into it. I read it out loud as I lay under my comforter.

"Opportunity for what? Splinters?" I whisper as I turn off my lamp. I close my eyes and wait for sleep.

A bright light wakes me. I thought I turned off my lamp? I sit up in bed, confused, until I see that the light is coming from the strange box!

The inscription on the box is *glowing*. The top blows open as the key shoots out, floating in midair. I know I should scream, but I'm too freaked to get any sound out!

The key continues floating in the air, and a glowing golden circle of light appears in the middle of my room. It shines so brightly that I have to shield my eyes. When the light dims, I can finally open them—but I'm still not sure they're working like they used to.

A door that looks like it's made out of solid gold has appeared from out of nowhere!

The key zooms toward the door and inserts itself into the keyhole. This is all too impossibly weird. I wish my room wasn't on the second floor so I could escape out my window.

There's a knock coming from the other side of the door. I yelp and shake my head. Am I awake? Or am I dreaming all this up because I had too much coffee ice cream for dessert?

I hear muffled words coming from behind the door. It's a gentle voice and I can't make out what they're saying.

This kind of thing doesn't happen in real life! I mean, this kind of thing might happen on *The Woodchuck Brigade*, when they battle the villainous reptile wizard the Chameleon, but that's television! I look around my room to see if Caruso the Chipmunk was going to tell his gang it's transforming time, but again, TV show.

Another knock comes from the door. This time it's a little faster and more urgent. I get out of my bed and slowly try to edge past the strange door. Hopefully I can book it out of my room before anything terrible happens. But then I hear the voice again.

This time it's a little louder. I can hear the words *any day now* and *turn the key*. I look to see where the voice is coming from, but when I check behind the door, there's nothing there.

I know it must lead to somewhere.

The knocking is soft and slow but constant.

"Who's there?" I ask. I realize I'm in some kind of twisted knock-knock joke come to life.

"Your lucky day," the voice sings. The voice sounds feminine and young—like someone my age. "If you turn the key, I'll be happy to show you."

"How do I know you're not a demon or a monster or a tax auditor or something?" I feel like a jerk that I'm buying into this. I also don't know what a tax auditor does, but it seems to be the kind of job grown-ups get nervous about.

"I assure you I am not interested in participating in any nefarious behavior." The music is now out of the stranger's voice, replaced with impatience. "Which begs the question, why would you summon me if you weren't going to open the door?"

"Summon you?" I ask.

"You read the inscription on the box, yes?"

I look over my shoulder. The words on the box are still ablaze in golden light.

"You promise you're not evil?" I ask, which is silly because of course an evil monster or tax auditor could just lie.

"My dear, if anything, I am going to bring you such good fortune, you'll never want me to leave. Now be a darling and turn the key. Let's get this show on the road, as it were."

I look down at the glowing key. Well, even if this does end in disaster, at least I'll have a story to tell at school. *Did you hear about Lila Moradi? Some magical space alien visited her in the middle of the night. Maybe we should ask her to join our a capella group?*

I put my index finger on the key and am relieved it's not hot to the touch, despite the way it's burning bright. I take a deep breath and turn it.

There's a creak, and the door busts open. The force pushes me backward. I land on my backside and look up to find a beautiful young kid wearing a sparkling gold dress gliding out of the doorway. Before I get a chance to see what else might come through the door, it slams shut and vanishes in a cloud of purple smoke. I cough as I look around, trying to figure out where it went.

"Finally," the visitor wearing the shiny dress says. "I was beginning to think you wouldn't answer. I'm glad I had the foresight to do away with that only-knocking-once policy."

"What happened to the door?" I ask, my voice cracking a little.

"Not to worry. It'll be back in seven days' time. That's how long we have together." The magical kid's dark brown eyes stare at me and widen in excitement. For some reason, their eyes don't look like they belong to someone my age. They look . . . like they've seen some things way beyond my years. A few tiny wrinkles at the corners give their face a sophisticated appearance. The kid has hair like mine, black, long, and curly, but it looks windswept and in control at the same time, like the way pop stars do at an awards show. "How novel! You're a child!"

"So are you," I say after I stop coughing. "Hang on a second. How . . . who . . . what is happening?"

"I've never been a child before! Usually, I find myself helping adults, which is frankly so uninspiring. They're always so obsessed with power and . . . well, romantic entanglements that you needn't worry about. Would you be so kind as to hand me a mirror, so I can see what I look like this time around?"

This time around?

"Whoa—who are you?" I ask. I'm whispering so I don't wake up my family.

"You don't need to speak in hushed tones. I've made sure that no one outside this room can hear us at the moment." The stranger imitates my whisper before speaking in a regular tone of voice again. "I'll answer all your questions in due time. But first: a mirror, please. What is your name, my dear?"

"I'm Lila Moradi," I say, mad at myself for standing up and walking to my dresser to bring a hand mirror to my accidentally invited guest.

"Lee-lah," they say as they gaze at themselves in the mirror. "I look spectacular. I'm so young! And beauteous! Look at my gorgeous eyebrows! I take it you're of Persian extraction, by the way you pronounce your name? A rich culture full of poetry and literature. It was quite the empire before Alexander the Great got ahold of my abilities. You're speaking colloquial North American English, so we're either in the States or Canada, yes? Oh, this is going to be such fun! How old are we?"

"What's this *we* business?" I ask, crossing my arms.

"As is a part of my duties, I take on the traits of whomever I am meant to aid. It helps me *blend in* so to speak. Though, if I am being honest, how can someone as fabulous as myself ever really blend in?" The guest grins, but I keep staring like they're speaking a language no one on Earth has ever heard of. "I have to say, this is not quite the warm welcome I was expecting. You called me; surely you know who I am?"

I don't know at all. I'm not quite sure they're human, even if they look like they are.

"You did summon me, didn't you?" the stranger asks. "You read the little rhyme, turned the key? The whole enchilada, as it were?"

I gulp. All I did was read the silly poem on the box. I wasn't expecting whatever this is!

"My, my. This *is* a first! Typically, I require no intro-duction. Not to be a bother, but how do we identify? Or rather, how do *you* identify, so that I'm able to do the same."

"Uh, I'm eleven," I say. "My pronouns are she/her, and again, WHO ARE YOU AND WHY WAS THERE A

WEIRD DOOR IN MY ROOM THAT JUST DISAPPEARED?"

The stranger tosses the hand mirror in the air . . . and it floats back to where it was on the dresser! She takes my hands in hers. At first, I worry my palms are clammy, but she doesn't seem to notice as she twirls us around.

"We're just a couple of girls who want to have fun," she says as we spin. She lets me go after a few turns and I land on my bed. "What a marvelous identity for us to share. During our time together, you may call me Felise." She gives me a radiant smile. I notice she has really great posture and seems very comfortable in her body. Mom says I need to stop slouching and walk with my shoulders back and my head held high, but I always forget. "To put it in terms that a child your age might understand—I am your lucky day."

"I'm not a little kid," I say, feeling really frustrated. That's the second time someone treated me like one in less than twenty-four hours. "Wait, my lucky day?"

"Yes. You have come across the key. I have no doubt you went to great lengths to find it."

"I don't get it," I say. Felise sits next to me on the bed and I inch away. She chuckles a little, instead of looking insulted.

"Please don't be frightened," she says sweetly. "I'm bound to help you. Those are the terms of my position." She's close to me and smells like all my favorite scents put together: pineapple, grass after a rainstorm, and the "berries" in Cap'n Crunch cereal. It calms me down, but I wonder . . . how does she smell like those things? Did she somehow know they are scents I like?

"Your position? Like a job?" I ask. Felise nods. "Are you, like, a fairy godmother or—?"

She throws her head back and laughs, and I can see all her perfectly shaped teeth. Felise doesn't need braces like my dentist says I will in a year or two.

"Fairy godmother. How droll." She wipes the corner of her eye with her pinky. "They do have better publicity, I'll give them that. Unfortunately, that is a false equivalence, as fairy godmothers aren't real. Perhaps they were created in storybooks to explain things your little human hearts can't quite accept. My dear, I am a very singular and elusive figure. Over the centuries, some have called me Fortuna, Providence, Lady Luck...I am Opportunity and I've knocked for you, you adorable so-and-so."

Felise extends her arms out to either side of her like she's a game show host telling me I've just won a new car. Then she lowers her arms, placing one hand on her hip. "To put it plainly, with me by your side, I can help you get what you want. It's one of my special powers! Surely there must be things that you want?" I nod but I still don't believe her. "Well, then, I can make sure those wants become reality by bestowing upon you the gift of *luck*."

I bite my lip, unsure if I should share my hopes and dreams with someone I just met—someone who can make objects float. I don't tell her that I wish I felt I belonged somewhere, with lots of friends who understood me. Instead, I tell her something that isn't so private.

"Could you help me save the music program at my school?" I ask her. She nods with enthusiasm.

"Should be child's play!" she says, then winces. "Ah—excuse me, pardon the expression. This is going to be such a lark of a week! Now, where will I be retiring for the evening?" Felise blinks her beautiful long eyelashes at me, as though all this is totally normal.

"You think I'm going to let someone who came through a strange magical door hang out here?" I ask. Though, weirdly, I realize I'm not scared of her. I have a feeling that has something to do with her *powers* or whatever.

"Of course. Besides, the door won't return until a week from now. Your luck will have changed by then— I'll make sure of it." Felise laughs, chipper as can be. "As a word of caution . . . I would hold on to that key if I were you. We wouldn't want it to get into the wrong hands."

Felise nods her chin toward the bronze key now lying on the floor. I get off the bed and pick it up. Now that it isn't glowing anymore, it seems even duller than it was when I first saw it. It vanishes out of my hands and my neck feels a little heavier. I discover a new necklace is looped around it. I hold it up to find the key, smaller in size than when I held it, dangling from a gold chain. I don't like wearing jewelry; I find it uncomfortable. But when I try to look for a clasp to undo it, I can't find one.

When I turn around, Felise is somehow wearing silk peach-colored pajamas and scooching under the covers of my bed!

"You don't mind if I bid you good night right away, do you?" she asks. "I've had such a long journey." Before I have a chance to answer, she's already made herself comfortable.

"How'd you change so fast?" I ask. I look for the dress she was wearing a second ago, but can't find it anywhere in the room.

"Remember the bit where I spoke to you about powers?" she asks me. Felise snaps her fingers and an eye mask appears on her forehead. My mouth drops open. "I told you. My abilities are *the real thing*! You'll see more of what I can do for you after we've both enjoyed a good night's sleep. I'm so excited for you to have me in your life!"

"Uh-huh, and don't worry about me. I've got a sleeping bag," I say with sarcasm. She doesn't pick up on it.

"A sleeping bag," Felise says with a dreamy look. "That

brings back memories of assisting a hiking troop on an expedition up Mount Everest." She slides her mask from her forehead to cover her eyes. "Now get some rest. We have a full day tomorrow. From this moment forward, the world is your oyster!" Felise yawns and settles into my bed.

I clutch the key hanging from my new necklace and wonder . . . *What have I gotten myself into?*

Chapter Four

I wake up to the sound of birds chirping and gentle music drifting in the air. I don't remember those noises being a part of my alarm clock options. I lift my head off the floor and find two lovebirds perched on my open windowsill, serenading me like I'm some sort of fairy-tale princess. The music comes from a small harp on my bedside table. The strings are vibrating on their own and the birds seem to be singing along with its tune. My bed is made perfectly, as though nobody slept in it. I take that as a good sign. Whatever happened last night must have been part of some dream.

Then again, the birds start to tweet out one of my

favorite pop songs. Maybe Felise really was here.

After I shower and get dressed, I walk downstairs and hear laughter coming from the kitchen. My mom and dad are letting out real belly laughs, but I can't imagine there's anything that funny on one of those morning TV shows. Especially since they stopped letting wild animals interact with the anchors, after the badger incident. (You don't want to know. I watched it one morning before school and didn't have any appetite for the rest of the day.)

I enter the kitchen to find Mom sitting next to Felise at the table. My dad is standing by the island, packing my lunch.

"Good morning!" Dad says in between laughs, trying to catch his breath. "Felise told us the funniest story. You've got to hear her tell it!"

"I do?" I ask, blinking at him faster than I've ever blinked before. "You . . . you can see her?"

Dad's laughter quiets down a little as he gives me a curious look.

"Come and eat breakfast before it gets cold," Mom says. There's a plate of blueberry pancakes on the table next to Felise. Usually on school days, I grab a granola bar as I head out, but I guess the birds woke me early enough that there's time for a stack of flapjacks.

I sit in the chair next to Felise but slide away from her a little. She doesn't seem to mind as she takes a sip of juice.

"It was so kind of you to serve fresh-squeezed orange juice this morning, Mrs. Moradi," Felise says to Mom.

"It's no trouble at all. We love having you over." Mom says it like Felise is over at our house all the time. "It was a good thing I found oranges in the refrigerator. I can't believe I didn't notice them before."

That's because we didn't *have* oranges in the refrigerator yesterday. I definitely would have noticed during my afternoon kitchen raid. I stare at Felise and she just takes another sip of her juice. Dad brings over my lunch box with my name on it and a glittery gold lunch box with Felise's name written in faded cursive.

"You packed her a lunch?" I ask, panicking a little. Mom and Dad look at me like I've said something really rude.

"We always pack Felise a lunch," Dad says.

"Since when?" I ask.

"Since . . ." Dad looks at Mom, his eyebrows coming together as he tries to remember.

"Well, since always," Mom says with a shrug.

"Sometimes a great friend can feel like they were always a part of your life, even before you met them," Felise says. She beams at my parents before turning to me. "You haven't touched your breakfast yet. You better hurry, we don't want to be late for school."

"There's no way you're coming to school with me!" I yell.

"Lila!" Mom and Dad say in unison.

"It's quite all right," Felise says to my parents, holding her hands up above her head and then lowering them, palms down, until they reach the table. My parents' shoulders and faces relax. "Lila and I have an extraordinary week ahead. Now eat up so you have energy for the day."

I stare down at my pancakes that already have syrup on them. The blueberries inside make the shape of a smiley face. The only times we ever have pancakes are on an occasional Sunday or on someone's birthday. I cut into them and the smell is incredible. I stab one with my fork but worry that maybe Felise has done something to my meal.

"I'm not hungry," I say.

"Pity," Felise says with a frown. "They're perfectly cooked with no additives."

"Of the magical variety?" I whisper. She nods. She could be lying, and I don't know what she's done to my parents to make them act like everything is rainbows and unicorns, but the pancakes do smell really good. I take a bite and they are fluffy and sweet. It's like eating a cumulonimbus cloud made of maple sugar and berries.

Parisa whizzes by, her backpack in one hand as she grabs a banana from the fruit bowl.

"I'm in a rush," Parisa says. "There's a student government meeting this morning."

"Wait," I say, my mouth full, crumbs spitting out of me. I want to see if she notices that something is *off* about this morning.

"Eww, gross," Parisa says, stopping in her tracks.

"Felise, tell your friend to chew with her mouth closed."

I guess Felise is more a part of the family than I realized.

�butterflies✿

I keep trying to get away from Felise on my walk to school, but whenever I turn around, she's right behind me. She doesn't even break a sweat to keep up.

"You really shouldn't be so skittish," she says. "I'm here to help you."

"You did something to my family!" I shout over my shoulder. "How come they all know you?" Then I face forward and find her standing in front of me. "Gah! How'd you do that?"

"Perhaps I wasn't as comprehensible as I should have been," she says. She clears her throat. "You invited me. I have arrived and I will be by your side for the next seven days."

"Look, I'm sorry. I didn't mean to invite you. Can we just forget the whole thing?" Yet even as I ask this, a butterfly gently lands on her perfectly tousled hair.

"Hospitality is evidently not your strong suit." Felise

holds out her pinky finger and the butterfly hovers over to it. "Sometimes when we're presented with gifts, it's good form to accept them *graciously.*" She points her pinky with the butterfly on it in my direction and it flutters over to my shoulder. The insect flaps its brightly colored yellow wings with orange flecks. I can't help but smile, even if Felise is freaking me out. "I wish no harm upon your family and friends," she says. "I'm simply doing my best to make my presence not so noticeable. If that requires a little magic on my end to put others at ease, well, so be it. After our time together, they won't be any wiser to my having been here."

"So let me get this straight: For the next seven days, even if I really don't want you to do anything or come with me to school, you, um, well, you're—"

"To put it in terms your sweet, not-fully-developed mind may grasp . . . you're stuck with me, kiddo." Felise says this with a hint of sass before going back to her gentle tone again. "This is meant to be a fortuitous occasion! My goodness, you act as if you've been bestowed some curse. That only happens if I don't go through the door with the key on the seventh day. I'm beginning to take offense. I mean, really, when all those men invoked my power they were so tiresome, but this is—"

"Wait, there's a curse?" I ask. Another butterfly lands on my arm.

"*Curse* is such a heavy word. More like repercussions. As some of your predecessors weren't so keen on letting me go after seven days, they found whatever luck I bestowed upon them was countered with a greater amount of misfortune. They also found that if the key was claimed by someone who had *not* summoned me, their luck changed for the worse."

It's the first time I've seen Felise look uneasy. Her eyes drift off, like she's recalling some terrible memory. I remember the necklace, grab it, and clutch the key tightly. That's why Felise told me to keep it with me at all times.

"But since you seem *so* eager to see me go," she says, "I doubt we'll have that issue. As long as I go through the door with the key when I'm meant to, it's only good luck for you and the residents of this fine little hamlet."

"Trust me, I don't think you have to worry about

extending your stay," I say. I take a deep breath. Felise winces a little. I realize that maybe I'm being rude. This isn't really her fault. It's mine for bringing the stupid box home. "Those pancakes *were* really good," I admit.

"Wasn't it lucky that your father was inspired to make them once he took a look at the blueberries he happened to find in the refrigerator?" Felise winks as the two of us continue our walk to school, side by side. "Oh, look!" She points at a twenty-dollar bill lying on the sidewalk in front of us. She picks it up and hands it to me. I look around to see if anyone may have dropped it, but it doesn't seem like it.

"Wow, you work fast," I say. I think this can be the initial donation to the fund to save the music program.

"You just wait and see," she says, linking her arm with mine. "I'm just warming up!"

Chapter Five

"It's so wonderful to attend a place of learning," Felise says. She stands ahead of me and gazes up at Providential Hills Middle School. "Think of the young people who will determine the future of civilization for years to come, all here in one space! All they require to succeed are nurturing educators, a curriculum to inspire curiosity, and a bit of luck to help shape their destinies."

I try to speak, but my words come out muffled.

Felise turns around. "Pardon? I didn't quite catch that."

I'm covered in butterflies from head to toe. There are so many on my face that they get in the way of what I'm trying to say. I twitch a few off my lips and it gives me enough time to shout. "Get them off!"

"I thought they made you smile?" Felise snaps her fingers and a weight lifts off me all at once. When I look up, there are hundreds of them floating up into the sky and breaking apart from one another as though being tossed in the wind. "Was that a little much?"

"Just a little!" I say, my eyes bulging out of my face. I can still feel their little legs tickling me. I shimmy to make sure there aren't any left on me.

"I'm sorry," she says. "I do get carried away when excited."

I trudge toward Felise, but it's hard to stay mad when she looks like a kid finding out about the tooth fairy for the first time. Better not to bring them up in front of Felise. I'd hate for her to tell me the tooth fairy wasn't real. Parisa told me it was Mom and Dad, but I don't buy it. My parents would absolutely have woken me up if they tried to slip money under my pillow. They'd have oohed and aahed at how cute I was when I slept. Nowadays they don't ooh and aah as much. I guess I'm not as cute anymore, but they do still give me hugs, which is nice.

We walk into school and there are students rushing to get stuff from their lockers before heading off to homeroom.

"Hello!" Felise waves to Cassandra Jean, a popular eighth grader on Melanie's soccer team who doesn't know I exist. I flinch, thinking Felise has embarrassed us and that Cassandra will pretend like she didn't hear her. Or give us a hairy eyeball.

"Hi, Felise," she says back, like it's the most natural thing in the world. "Hey, Lila."

"She knows my name?" I ask. I'm bewildered that I'm on the radar of a star student athlete who always knows what to wear to school dances and always has lots of friends around her, on and off the field.

"Why wouldn't she?" Felise asks. "You're a fabulous young person. When you're not so nervous about everything." We walk into homeroom where we all have assigned desks.

"Good morning, Lila," Ms. Zeller says without any enthusiasm. She's a good teacher for homeroom and she's fair, but she's not really warm. Ms. Zeller doesn't smile a lot but that's okay, I guess. It takes all kinds or whatever. The only time I've seen her laugh was during morning announcements when Jimmy said a hyena escaped from a zoo and ended up in his backyard, and there was so much commotion when animal control came that he didn't have time to do his homework. She said it was the most creative excuse she'd heard yet.

"Good morning, Ms. Zeller," I say. I wait for her to ask who my friend is.

"Good morning, Felise," Ms. Zeller says. She acts like Felise has been a part of her class since September, like the rest of us.

"Ms. Zeller, always a pleasure," Felise says. "And might I add that cardigan looks smashing on you."

"Thank you," Ms. Zeller says without a hint of a smile, but her eyes brighten. "Take your seats, the bell is about to ring."

I look at my desk and, lo and behold, there's a brand-new one next to mine that wasn't there before. Felise gets comfortable at her sparkling-clean desk, which isn't dinged up or scratched like the rest of ours. I sit at my desk. The initials of previous students who sat here are carved into the wood. I wait for someone, anyone, to question who Felise is and why she's here. Nobody seems to notice a thing. It's just another regular day.

"This is so exciting!" Felise says, pulling out a notebook from inside her desk and a pen with a golden pom-pom on top of it. The notebook has her name written in cursive across the front. If Felise really is Lady Luck personified and has spent eons in the universe around incredible people, I can't understand why she'd think Ms. Zeller's homeroom class is going to be all that thrilling.

"Hey, Lila," Melanie says, walking to her desk, which is right in front of mine. "Will I see you at our game today? You don't have to come if you don't want to. I have a feeling we're going to lose big-time."

"Melanie! Hi!" I say, relieved to see her. "Do you notice anything unusual about today?" I ask. I tilt my head not-so-subtly toward Felise. Melanie looks at Felise and squints. At last, someone will notice that Felise isn't meant to be here!

"Did you get a haircut, Felise?" Melanie asks.

"Absolutely not! Why would I mess with perfection?

What a question." Felise sways her hair from side to side so it bounces like in a shampoo commercial. I slump in my seat as the bell rings. Everyone sits at their desks and quiets down. Melanie faces me and rolls her eyes.

"Looks like Felise is in one of her moods again," Melanie whispers to me. I can't take it anymore. I stand up and everyone in class, including Ms. Zeller, stares at me.

"Isn't anybody going to ask who Felise is?" I plead with my peers. There are a couple of giggles, and some kids whisper among themselves.

"Felise is a member of our class," Ms. Zeller says matter-of-factly. She smooths out the bottom of her cardigan with her hands. "An integral part at that."

"What's integral mean?" I ask, still standing. I realize that everyone is staring at me like I've asked the dumbest question in the world, even though Ms. Zeller says there are no dumb questions. Felise raises her hand.

"I can answer that, Ms. Zeller," Felise says. Ms. Zeller nods her head. Felise lowers her hand and addresses the class, making eye contact with almost everyone around her. Her shoulders are straight, her chin is out, and she looks like she's one of those important diplomats who give speeches at United Nations summits. "The dictionary defines *integral* as an adjective meaning essential or fundamental, but for our purposes, it means I am phenomenal and very important to this homeroom setting."

"Don't you think it's weird that she talks like that?" I ask my friends. I can tell I'm losing them by the way they raise their eyebrows or try to hold in a laugh. I sit down in defeat. I guess Felise is right in that no one will be the wiser about who she is or where she came from. It's still annoying, though.

"Now that we've all settled in," Ms. Zeller says, which is her way of saying *no more zany outbursts or interruptions please*, "I was going to give you a pop quiz on our lesson yesterday."

The class groans and so do I. I didn't study much last night, except about who Mr. Mammonton is.

"Then I gave it some thought," Ms. Zeller says. "And, well, you've all been working so hard. I thought we'd spend morning period watching a short film about dinosaurs."

The class cheers as Ms. Zeller pushes the remote on the projector and asks Jimmy to turn off the lights. Ms. Zeller *never* has us watch anything in class, even when it's right before vacation and most other classes goof off or watch a movie until it's time to go home.

I look over at Felise. She wiggles in her seat, making herself comfortable to kick back and enjoy the film.

"Don't worry," Felise whispers to me. "I'll make sure *all* your desks are upgraded like mine before the week is over."

I lean back in my chair, still shocked that she's getting away with being here. I stare at the projected brontosaurus chewing on leaves. I should ask Felise where she was when the asteroid struck. The dinosaurs could have used a lot of luck too.

Chapter Six

"So do people need you to visit them to be a lucky person?" I ask as I push buttons on the vending machine. My parents never pack me a dessert unless it's fruit, which they say is nature's candy but I say doesn't count. The candy bar I select gets stuck between the metal rings and doesn't drop like it's supposed to.

"Not necessarily," Felise says. "Luck is what you make of it." She watches me shake the machine, but I'm unable to move the candy bar all that much. "Bad luck happens to good people sometimes and good luck happens to bad people sometimes, but belief in oneself and taking chances one otherwise wouldn't can impact someone's fortune. There's really only so much *I* can do. What people do with their good fortune is up to them."

I kick the vending machine a few times, then bump it with my hip. The candy bar doesn't budge.

"May I?" She doesn't wait for me to answer and snaps her fingers. All the chips, crackers, cookies, and chocolate bars fall down at the same time. They pour out of the door flap at the bottom of the vending machine. Felise hands me a tote bag that she didn't have in her hands a moment ago. "The luckiest people, of course, are those who have good friends."

"Uh-huh," I say, staring down at the pile of junk food. "Thanks, but I only needed the one bar."

"As I mentioned, I do have a tendency to overdo it when I'm excited," she says with a laugh. "I'll help you pack it up." She twirls her finger in the air and the bags of chips and cookies start to float upward in midair.

"No!" I say, swatting the food to the floor. I look over my shoulder to see if anyone spots candy flying in the air. "I'll take care of it." I bend down and start filling the tote bag with goodies. "I thought the idea was to blend in?"

"One can blend in and stand out at the same time," Felise says. She bends down and starts to pack along with me. "But I suppose you're right. We don't want my being here to cause any alarm. Or have anyone else try to exploit my powers on *your* time. I'm here only for you, of course."

"I'm honored," I say with a hint of sarcasm. She doesn't pick up on it and flashes me a toothy grin.

🦋🦋🦋

"What is this incredible room?" Felise asks as she sniffs the air and looks at kids sitting at long tables.

"This is the cafeteria," I say. I hold my lunch box in one hand and the heavy tote bag full of snacks in the other. I guess she never helped any students or teachers in her long luck-giving career.

"How quaint! A room for lunches! Where should we sit?" Felise asks. "Over by Melanie?"

Melanie is eating at a table with her soccer team-mates. They usually sit together on game days. She never said I couldn't sit with them, but all they talk about is soccer. I don't feel like I have much to add to that conversation other than I think we should call it football like the rest of the world does. But I know that's an unpopular opinion.

"Maybe not today," I say as I look for a place we can sit alone.

"What about them? They look like a friendly bunch." Felise nods at a table where Carolina, Veronica, and some other band kids who are really good at music but don't put in much effort are sitting. I mean, I *know* Carolina and Veronica, but I'm not super friendly with them and they haven't exactly invited me to eat with them. Before I can explain any of this to Felise, she walks ahead of me to their table.

"May we join you?" Felise asks.

"Sure," Carolina says and scooches down the bench so there's room for the two of us. Felise makes it look so easy to go up and talk to people. She sits down right away and pats a spot on the bench next to her for me to join.

"Would anyone like a snack?" Felise asks. "Lila has some additional sustenance to share."

I plop the tote bag on the table and most of the snacks spill out.

"Wow! Thanks, Lila," Veronica says, taking a bag of chips. "Going to need something to eat on mystery meat day." Everybody picks something from the vending machine haul and thanks me. There's still enough food for me to pass out to my whole class this afternoon and tomorrow. I take the candy bar I wanted and save it for dessert.

"What exactly is mystery meat?" Felise asks, her eyes wide with interest rather than revulsion.

"That's the mystery," Veronica says. She sticks her fork into the meat mixture and swirls it around. "I wish it was pizza day, but we haven't had pizza in a really long time."

"Pizza! Yes!" Felise shouts out a little too loudly. Kids at other tables turn their heads to watch her. "The last time I had pizza was in Silicon Valley in the eighties. Were it not for pizza sustaining the employees, Atari may not have become one of the greatest companies of all time." Veronica and Carolina stare at her, unsure of what she's talking about. "You're welcome for Atari by the way."

"What's Atari?" Carolina asks.

"So, Carolina," I say, trying to change the subject because I don't know what Atari is either. It's a part of Felise's past lives, and the less people know about those, the better. "How long have you been playing piano? You're really talented."

"Oh, thank you." Carolina looks a little embarrassed. "I asked my mom if I could learn to play when I was really little. I started lessons when I was five."

"Were you always so good?" I ask as I open my lunch box. "I mean, I'm sure it takes a lot of practice to be as good as you are, but did it come naturally to you?"

Carolina thinks about this a moment before she answers.

"I've always loved playing," she says seriously. "But sometimes I wish it didn't take up so much of my time."

"I know what you mean," Veronica says, no longer bothering with the cafeteria's mystery meat and chowing down on vending machine chips instead. "I don't *love* flute, but my parents think if I keep playing it's going to lead to me playing in the symphony or something."

"I guess you'll have more time for other things when band is over," I say. I look down at what Dad packed for me. Koofteh meatball in a pita with scallions, string cheese, grapes, and a clementine. There's a note inside too that says *Don't forget, you're our sunshine.* I try to hide the note, but Felise sees it. She doesn't read it aloud, but she does smile.

"I do like band," Carolina says. "Mr. Hernandez isn't as strict as my other instructors. It's more fun than my music commitments outside school. Band isn't as serious."

"You mean amateur hour," Veronica says, in kind of a mean way. Then I guess she remembers I'm in band too. "Sorry, Lila. I didn't mean . . . it's just not so competitive."

"I get it," I say. I'm not offended. I am an amateur. I only wish there was something I was as passionate about as Carolina is about piano. Though from the way Veronica plays, she's an amateur too. "I love listening to music, but I don't know if I'm cut out to play it."

"Nonsense," Felise says. "I am sure you are an excellent musician. What instrument do you play?" Carolina and Veronica avert their eyes and look humiliated for me.

"The triangle," I say. Felise stares at me blankly, but I can see the gold glint in her eyes fade a little.

"I do have my work cut out for me," Felise murmurs. I take a bite of my sandwich. I don't know how Felise did it, but the koofteh is still warm.

❋ ❋ ❋

The Providential Hills Clovers soccer team is losing 2–0 to the Deerwood Jaguars when Felise and I join the few fans watching the game from the bleachers. Melanie is out on the field. The ribbons in her hair look as frayed as she is.

"What if we went to a casino?" I ask Felise. I'm trying to think of more ways to save the school's music program.

"Perish the thought," Felise says, making a face of disgust. "Casinos are incredibly depressing. There's never any natural light in there and you can feel the despair radiating off the walls. I do, however, enjoy a buffet. Besides, the house always wins. Everyone knows that."

"I guess I'm too young to gamble anyway," I say. I'm kind of relieved. Those slot machines look sort of fun, but I don't know much about cards and I definitely don't have a poker face. Mom always knows when I'm lying or having a bad day and trying to hide it from her. I'm trying to work on it.

"Don't you worry," Felise says. "We'll make sure your cohort of merry musicians can continue their melodic pursuits. For the time being, let's enjoy the game." A player on the other team dribbles the ball toward our goal. Melanie runs to the ball and manages to kick it out of bounds. "Woo! Well done, Melanie!" Felise shouts, but she's the only one cheering. As great as Melanie and her teammates are, they have yet to win a game this season. "Will we celebrate with Melanie after the game?"

"I don't know if they're going to be in a celebrating mood," I say, looking at the scoreboard. There are only ten minutes left. "And celebrating is team stuff."

"Supporters are an important part of the team," Felise says. "Let's cheer on Melanie together! No matter the outcome, you still want to show your friend you support her, don't you?"

She's right. Even if we don't win, it's good to know

that people care. I hope there's an audience for our band concert. I know my family and Melanie will be there, even if I won't have that much to do. Melanie will for sure root for me.

"Come on, defense! Get that ball out of there!" I yell out. When one of the Jaguar players kicks the ball at our goal, it goes too high, hits the top crossbar, and bounces into the air. Everyone on the field watches the ball as it flies over their heads near the other goal. Cassandra runs, beats the defenders to the ball, and kicks it past the Jaguars' goalie.

I jump up and clap my hands as Cassandra's teammates huddle around her to pat her on the back.

"Two to one, we're almost there," Felise says. "Let's keep up our school spirit, shall we?"

"Let's go, Clovers!" I scream out. The other fans around me follow my lead and keep the chant going as the forwards kick for possession of the ball in the center of the field. The chant continues when Cassandra kicks the ball to Melanie. "Go, Mel, Go! Kick it in the goal!"

She kicks the ball from half field. It looks like she was

passing it to Amaya Thompson, but a sudden gust of wind blows the ball with the force of a tornado to the inside of the goal, before the Jaguars' goalie even notices it hitting the net. The small crowd starts to sound like a much bigger one. I look around to see more students who were walking by pause to watch the game.

"Two to two. How about that!" Felise claps in time with the chanting fans.

"Are you, um . . . ?" I begin to ask if she has something to do with how well the Clovers are doing. Felise acts like she didn't hear me. She marches down to the front of the bleachers and looks up at our cheering section.

"Come on, everyone!" Felise commands. "Let's show our Clovers some appreciation!" She releases a "Huzzah!" when everyone starts to cheer louder than I think is humanly possible. Felise joins me at my side again as the Jaguars advance to our defensive line.

"DE-FENSE! DE-FENSE!" I yell out. The fans do the same. We are a chorus devoted completely to the Clovers. There's something powerful about being part of a group, leading them in something bigger than just us. I don't get that from playing in band, but I'd love to have this feeling with me as much as possible. Does this mean I should join cheerleading? I'm not so sure, but I do know that I like feeling a part of things. I want to help in some way, even if it's by doing something small like encouraging a friend.

The referee calls something out that I can't hear because the growing number of fans drowns their voice out.

"Two-minute warning," Felise says. "Plenty of time."

When she says that, it feels like time literally slows down. The players move quickly, but the seconds on the clock drag on as though each one was five. Even the crowd seems to be cheering in slow motion, like they're on some instant replay slo-mo camera for an audience *elsewhere*. The Clovers and Jaguars keep playing at their usual speed. Cassandra heads the ball to Melanie and she dribbles it near the Jaguars' goal. A Jaguar defender slides in front of Melanie, trips her, and she falls hard onto the turf.

"Oh no!" I say. Melanie stays splayed out on the grass. The crowd goes quiet, hoping she gets up soon.

Melanie slowly raises herself up, her teammates checking in to make sure she's not injured. She just brushes herself off and waves at us. The crowd goes wild, hooting and hollering. Time goes back to feeling how it always did. I look up to see there are only three seconds left on the game clock.

"Penalty kick!" the ref yells out and sets up the ball for Melanie. The Clovers line up behind her for support and the crowd quiets down.

"You can do this," I whisper.

The Jaguars' goalie looks ready to pounce on the ball wherever Melanie kicks it.

Melanie takes a deep breath. The ref blows the whistle. Melanie runs up to the ball and kicks it to the top right corner of the goal. The goalie doesn't get there in time, but it looks like the ball is about to hit the goalpost! Until a tricky gust of wind corrects its direction and it heads straight into the net.

"We won!" I yell. I hop up and down. Melanie's teammates huddle around and hug her. The fans and I whoop and jump and make all kinds of noise.

"It's time to celebrate!" Felise says. The Clovers and

Jaguars line up to slap hands and congratulate one another on a good game. Now, that's a tradition I like. I wish we could apply it to all competitions and tests. Like after a math quiz, even if I didn't do so well, I'd like Ms. Zeller to give me a high five and say "Good job" when I passed it in.

Felise marches down to the field. She stops on the grass and turns around to look for me. "Well, come on!" she shouts up at me. I rush down and join her, both of us walking toward Melanie.

"Great job, Melanie," I say when I see her. She gives me a hug.

"Thanks!" Melanie says as she lets me go. "And thanks for cheering! It meant a lot." She's smiling wide. Her white jersey is marked with grass stains, mud, and sweat. It's how a real soccer player's jersey looks after a well-fought battle.

"We must commemorate the occasion with some refreshments," Felise says. As soon as she does, I hear familiar jingling music in the parking lot at the end of the field. An ice cream truck stops right smack-dab in the parking lot by the field. It isn't even summertime.

The driver gets out of the musical truck, decorated with ice pops featuring *The Woodchuck Brigade* and other ice cream superheroes. I didn't know *The Woodchuck Brigade* had ice pops! (I try not to show my excitement about that in front of Melanie and Felise. It would be too nerdy.)

"Hey, kids!" the driver yells out. "My freezer busted and I've got some treats left over from the day. Can I interest you in any free slushies or ice pops?"

"I do prefer gelato," Felise says, "but then again, we're only on day one. I should cut myself some slack if things don't turn out exactly as I'd like them to."

Melanie looks at her, not understanding what Felise is talking about, but then puts her arm around my shoulders.

"Come on, let's eat with the team," Melanie says. "You too, Felise." The three of us walk to the ice cream truck. The tinkly music coming from the truck's speakers sounds like it's playing Queen's "We Are the Champions." For one afternoon, that's exactly how I feel. I'm a champion of the world!

Chapter Seven

I didn't have any homework because none of my teachers remembered to assign any all day. Another stroke of luck. This meant I had time to watch TV with my family, which now apparently included Felise, in the living room.

She complimented Mom on dinner. It wasn't anything special, just a rotisserie chicken ready-prepared from the grocery store, but I guess Felise hasn't had poultry in a while. I was surprised my mom didn't bring home lobsters or steaks, given Felise's supernatural influence, but I guess Felise's powers were used up for the day. That was fine by me. It had been a pretty stellar day. I loved joking around with Melanie,

Cassandra, and the rest of the team when we ate our slushies. (I did get a Caruso the Chipmunk, from *The Woodchuck Brigade*, ice pop, but I pretended like I was picking a random treat and it wasn't that a big deal. It was delicious and his red bubblegum nose was divine.)

Cassandra's really sweet and we found out we both like this anime show from Japan that I didn't think many people at school knew about. After today, it feels like it wouldn't be so weird to sit with Melanie and her teammates at lunch once in a while.

The meteorologist on TV shows the seven-day forecast. It's nothing but sunny days, without a cloud in sight. Perfect temperatures—not too hot, not too cold—for the rest of the week.

I turn to Felise, sitting next to me on the couch. She cups her face in her hands, raises her eyebrows, and bats her eyelashes with an *aren't I just the greatest* expression. I laugh until I hear what the local news anchor says next.

"The Providential Hills Bank has reported articles from a safe-deposit box missing as of yesterday," the anchor says. I feel like he's looking right at me when he says it. "The stolen item is an heirloom belonging to a bank customer who wishes to remain anonymous but is offering a generous reward to anyone with any information. No questions asked."

I start to feel a nervous ache in my stomach. It's like the ones I get before I have to take a big test or when I don't know what to say when a teacher calls on me.

"This is so boring," Parisa says, her legs dangling over the armrest at the end of the couch as she pushes buttons on her phone.

"How about we play a game?" Dad asks, turning off the TV. "Anyone up for backgammon?"

"No," Parisa says. She sits up and she has a devilish grin on her face. "Monopoly."

I groan. I think Mom internally does too when I see her close her eyes and grit her teeth. Monopoly goes on forever and Parisa takes it so seriously. It's no fun when everyone knows that Parisa always wins every game we ever play together as a family.

"I've never played that game before," Felise says with excitement.

"You're not missing a thing," I say.

Parisa's grin reminds me of the Grinch's in the Chuck Jones animated special, when the Grinch gets a horrible idea to ruin Christmas for the Whos. (Chuck Jones was a legendary cartoon director and his legacy will never fade.)

"I'd be happy to show you how to really play," Parisa says. She's got a flicker in her eyes that shows up during any competition she takes part in. I've always interpreted this look of hers to mean *I will destroy you.*

"Splendid," Felise says, intertwining her fingers and cracking her knuckles. "Let the games begin!"

"Looks like you landed on my property," Parisa says to me. "Pay up, buttercup!"

I hate when Parisa gets like this. She's already bankrupted our parents and I'm on my way to joining them soon. It isn't just that she wins that's so annoying, it's the way she *gloats* about it. Even though the Clovers won today, they didn't taunt the Jaguars or make them feel bad about the loss. I figured Parisa would have caught on to good sportsmanship, what with all the volleyball she supposedly plays.

"Here," I say, forking over my fake money. She counts every bill, one by one, slowly and with a sinister cackle.

"Some people just don't have the skills to pay the bills," Parisa says. She places the dollars on top of her already giant stack.

"Okay, Parisa, that's enough," Dad says as he brings over a bowl of popcorn for all of us to snack on.

"What?" Parisa asks. "I can't help it if none of you ever learn your lesson. You don't mess—"

"With the best," my parents and I all say together. Maybe Felise can magically make our Monopoly board disappear for good?

"I believe it is my turn," Felise says, reaching for the dice.

"Best of luck," Parisa says with a smirk. Felise doesn't respond. Instead, she raises one eyebrow and looks directly at Parisa when she lets go of the dice.

🦋🦋🦋

"Why, Lila! You've landed on the Chance square again!" Felise exclaims. Parisa looks frustrated as her stack of brightly colored cash is mostly gone.

"Huh! How about that?" I have to say I'm enjoying

beating Parisa at this game for once. I pick up a Chance card and read the good news aloud. I might not have "skills to pay the bills," but I have a truckload of luck. "It's your turn, Parisa."

My sister is still confident and grabs at the dice. She shakes them up really well, and when the dice fall, so does her face.

"Why, if the numbers are correct, that means you will land on the Go to Jail square," Felise says. "Oh dear. Well, I have no doubt you'll be released from there in no time."

Parisa doesn't yell or complain, but her right eye starts to twitch.

After I beat Parisa at Monopoly, she suggests we play the game of Life. When I win that, she says we should play Catan. When I win that, she proposes Clue. After I figure out it's Colonel Mustard in the study with a candlestick, Mom and Dad say they're tired and maybe it's time for all of us to call it a night. But Parisa demands we play Battleship. After I sink hers, she whips out UNO. When I win that, there's only one game left on the shelf and, well . . . things still don't go her way.

"Lila, you made it to Candy Castle!" Felise says, so loudly that my parents wake up from their naps on the couch. "What a whimsical journey we embarked upon. It is most unfortunate that you were mired in Molasses Swamp, Parisa."

"Good game," I say. I hold out my hand for Parisa to shake like I've done for all the other games we've played tonight. She doesn't look up at me or shake my hand, just keeps staring at the board. Her eyes look frantically back and forth at her game piece and mine.

"I . . . but I can't lose," Parisa says. "This is Candy Land! It's a game for babies!" She jabs her finger at the spaces, counting again to make sure I really did win, trying to trace her steps for what she did wrong. I take my hand back, realizing she's not in a mood to offer me congratulations.

"What time is it?" Mom asks, rubbing the sleep out of her eyes.

"Time for bed." Dad stands up and stretches. "Come on, ladies."

"No!" Parisa says. She pounds her fist on the table. I

shift away a little. "We can keep playing! Best of three. It'll be fun."

It doesn't feel fun anymore. It feels like Parisa is going through something she hasn't really experienced before. Loss. Felise yawns and covers her mouth with her hand.

"I am afraid it's past my bedtime," Felise says, standing up and lifting me up by my arm. She's a lot stronger than she looks. "See you tomorrow, everyone! Sleep well!"

"Good night, Felise joon! Good night, Lila joon!" Mom and Dad say. When we walk upstairs, I can hear Parisa's voice in the living room.

"But I thought like a winner," Parisa whimpers. It almost makes me wish Felise had let her win one of the games. Almost.

Felise brushes her teeth with a gold-colored toothbrush. I wouldn't be surprised if it's made of actual gold. She swishes the bristles across her mouth and builds up a froth so foamy it begins to drip down her chin, gross drool pooling at the bottom of the sink.

"That's not very ladylike," I say, brushing my own teeth with a plain white toothbrush. I got rid of my Bugs Bunny toothbrush because Parisa made fun of it, but I kind of wish I hadn't.

"I beg to differ," Felise says. "Ladies contain multitudes. There is no one way to be a lady." She spits a gob of toothpaste into the sink, then makes her voice sound exactly like Parisa's. "I just want to make sure I have a winning smile." I laugh a little, even if her ability to mimic my sister creeps me out. She seems to sense that and speaks again in the voice I'm used to. "Does your sister always behave in that manner?"

I nod. "Parisa's really good at most everything she tries. She's not used to things not going her way."

"I should say not," Felise says. She picks up a glass of water and takes a sip. Then she tilts her head back and gargles what I think is a song my mom likes: "I'm Every Woman." She then spits the water out in a perfect curve, like she's some kind of fountain statue. I laugh so hard I almost choke on my toothbrush. Felise wipes her mouth with the back of her hand. "Ahhh! That's minty fresh!"

I stop brushing and spit. I sip from my cup and try to spit out the water like she did, but it lands on the edge of the sink and water drips onto the floor. I can't even do that right! Good thing there isn't a spitting water club at school. I wouldn't make it in there either.

"That is quite all right. Accidents will happen," Felise says, noticing my disappointment. A hand towel floats off the hook on the wall and soaks up the small puddle at my feet.

"Accidents happen a lot for me," I say. "It's probably because I don't 'think like a winner,' like Parisa says I should."

"I shudder to think what other advice your dear sister has given you." Felise puts her toothbrush in a cup and picks up the floss. "It is good to be optimistic and give things your best effort, but people who are constantly trying to look on the sunny side without facing reality are tiresome. Besides, if we didn't have spills, towels would be obsolete. A world without towels, well, I don't know if it's one I want to roam around in."

That makes sense, I guess.

"You're so—"

"Magnificent? Charming? Astounding?"

"I was going to say weird," I mutter truthfully. She turns her nose up at that and sniffs the air. "But in a good way!" I add.

Felise smiles and I can't believe it, but . . . I'm starting to think she's pretty okay.

"Do you think tomorrow you could help me come up with ideas to fundraise for band?" I ask.

"Indubitably," Felise says, ripping off the perfect amount of floss from a gold container.

Chapter Eight

Day two of the Felise experience feels like any ordinary day, except for the pop quiz that happens in English class. Luckily I'm prepared, because Felise asked me to read from our assigned book to her before she went to sleep. In *my* bed, which was annoying, but my sleeping bag had been replaced with a futon. I couldn't figure out if Felise had done that or if one of my parents—who were more than happy to host Felise, no questions asked—took care of it.

Now I sit in band with my triangle in hand, giving Mr. Hernandez my full attention. I plan on not missing one cue. Felise is by my side, holding a case, but I can't tell what instrument she has inside it. Knowing her, she's probably stuffed a giant cello, which couldn't possibly fit, in there just to show off.

"Okay, everyone," Mr. Hernandez says from the front of the room. The metronome near him is clicking back and forth. "Let's take it from the top." He raises his hands above his head, signaling that we should all get ready. Veronica squeaks out a shrill note from her flute before Mr. Hernandez gives us the go-ahead.

"Sorry," Veronica says, sitting up straight in her seat and puckering her lips. Mr. Hernandez closes his eyes and counts to three, then opens his eyes and waves his hands for us to start. We don't sound too bad, but our version of Louis Armstrong's "What a Wonderful World" isn't so wonderful at all. It's a beautiful song, but if it weren't for Carolina's piano, we'd be mangling one of the greatest songs. It makes me wonder if Mr. Hernandez really thinks we can pull off a version that's acceptable for an audience to listen to. I'm still waiting for my cue when the blast of a saxophone overpowers all other sounds in the room. It rips the notes coming out of *our* instruments to shreds. Felise stands up—*she's* the one blowing into the alto sax. Her eyes are closed and she's completely engrossed in her own playing. I look around to see what everybody thinks. Jimmy has completely abandoned his oboe (which was bringing the mood of the song down) and gawks at Felise. Veronica's eyebrows are furrowed, and her fingers continue to go through the motions as she plays her flute, trying to keep up or outdo Felise. But I know that's not going to happen. Carolina looks lighter than I've ever seen her. She starts to play along. Both she and Felise go off book, playing a song that I don't recognize. They're improvising, riffing off each other like real jazz musicians do.

Mr. Hernandez doesn't stop Felise. Instead, he does something I've never seen him do before. He taps his foot! Felise opens her eyes—her cheeks puffed out like a blowfish—and raises her eyebrows at me. I point at myself, making sure it is me she wants to start playing. She nods. So, I hit my triangle when I feel like it and it does sound pretty good! Or maybe it doesn't, but it feels good to just play and not worry about if I'm going to miss my cue or if I'm messing up. Felise walks toward the piano and I do the same. Carolina keeps up with Felise's melody. I keep banging on my triangle, dancing along to the beat. Jimmy has put down his oboe and is thumping on his music case with his hands like he's playing a set of bongo drums.

The song crescendos (that's a word Mr. Hernandez likes to use a lot) and when it's almost over, everyone else stops playing except for Felise. She plays an incredible solo that doesn't overstay its welcome. When she finishes, she winks at me, and I do what I'm supposed to do. I hit the triangle.

Everybody cheers and claps except for Veronica. Mr. Hernandez looks really surprised.

"That was awesome!" Jimmy says, his oboe still lying on the chair next to him.

"It was okay," Veronica mutters, looking at the notes in front of her. "I didn't realize we were able to just go off book like that."

"It was so fun!" Carolina exclaims from her piano bench. I've never seen her so excited about being in band before. "To be able to *feel* a song instead of playing on command. We should be doing more of *that* when we're together."

Mr. Hernandez doesn't say anything, but he smiles.

Carolina doesn't usually get this animated in his class-room. I guess she didn't have a reason to if she wasn't having the greatest time.

"Yeah, we might as well enjoy band while we can," Jimmy says with a shrug. "Would it be okay if I switched to percussion instead of playing oboe?"

Mr. Hernandez doesn't have as fast an answer for that as Felise does.

"Certainly, it would be okay. Why wouldn't it be?" Felise's sax dangles from a strap around her neck. She looks so cool; she doesn't even need a pair of sunglasses or hat. (The coolest member of *The Woodchuck Brigade*, Kimbra the squirrel, has sunglasses and a hat. Although she doesn't play saxophone, which would be even cooler, but I digress.)

"My parents got me into oboe," Jimmy says.

"Have you told them you'd like to play something else?" Felise asks. Jimmy thinks about it, then shakes his head. "Would you suffer terrible consequences if you told them how you feel?"

"I mean not *terrible*, but you haven't met my mom," Jimmy says with a laugh. "She always wanted to play oboe when she was younger but couldn't afford lessons."

"Living vicariously through one's children," Felise says. "How antiquated."

"That's enough, Felise," Mr. Hernandez says. And I have to admit, I'm impressed. None of the other teachers have checked her yet. "Jimmy, I'm happy to talk to your parents with you if you'd like to switch instruments." Jimmy sits up a little taller in his seat. I hope it works out for him. "I agree that what you just performed was exceptional."

"Mostly the piano and saxophone," I say, because it's true.

"Nonsense," Felise interrupts me. "That song wouldn't have had nearly as much oomph or panache without the triangle." I don't think that's accurate, but it makes me blush anyway. "It would be a shame to see our jam sessions come to an end due to budgeting oversights."

"What if we had a bake sale?" Carolina asks. I don't know how many brownies or cookies we'd have to sell to keep band going for another semester, but it's a start! Mr. Hernandez folds his arms across his chest and rests against the edge of the desk behind him. This is his *I'm thinking* pose, but I don't think he knows that I've noticed that.

"I do make a great bran muffin," Veronica says. I have a feeling those aren't going to be bestsellers, but hey, at least Veronica is on board too.

"It would be a big undertaking," Mr. Hernandez says. "We'd have to raise at least twenty thousand dollars."

"Oh man, forget it," Jimmy says, throwing his hands up in the air. "There's no cake in the world that can bring in that much dough. Pun intended."

"We can at least try," Carolina says. "If we don't meet the mark, we can donate the money to a charity or another club at the school." Mr. Hernandez is still leaning on the desk. "Please, Mr. Hernandez. Today was really good. I haven't felt that way about playing in a long time." The way she says that makes me sad. I always thought if a person was good at something, it had to be because they loved it. I think Carolina hasn't loved playing the piano in a while. Maybe being good at something can kind of turn into an accidental trap?

The better you get at something, the more people expect you to always be good at it. I guess I didn't feel the weight of the pressure Carolina must be under until now.

Mr. Hernandez stands up straight and puts his hands on his hips. Superhero stance for a superhero decision. (I'm partial to the villains in comics, as they're more interesting. But nobody stands the way Superman and Wonder Woman do.)

"You know, I do make a decent scone," Mr. Hernandez says. "I'm willing to give it a shot if you all are?"

"Yes! We are!" I say and raise my hand. Everybody else follows. Maybe we *can* save band! The only problem is . . . well, I tried joining culinary club once. I added too much baking soda to a cake mixture. Nobody got food poisoning, but I wasn't asked back to learn how to bake focaccia. I'd been looking forward to it too. I love focaccia.

It was Felise's idea to come to the ShopTilYouDrop grocery store after school.

Melanie joins us since she doesn't have a game, which

is fun. What isn't fun is seeing all the items Felise is adding to her cart when I know my allowance won't cover it all. Felise picks up a bottle of truffle oil and puts it in the cart. I look at the price tag on the shelf and start to panic.

"Felise!" I say. "What do we need truffle oil for? I thought we were just going to make brownies from a box!" I pull the bottle out of the cart.

"I thought we might make something savory as well," Felise says, eyeing the bottle. "We need to give people options."

"Okay, but can we maybe come up with something that won't cost so much?" I put the truffle oil gently back on the shelf and inch away from it slowly. I don't want to break it and then have to buy it.

"I see your point," Felise says. "Though I really wish you wouldn't worry so. I am never going to steer you wrong." She holds out her fist for me to bump. I do, and out of some bizarre instinct, my hands start doing motions they've never done before, matching each of Felise's slaps and snaps and bumps like we've been greeting each other this way for years. We end the handshake with a hip check. Then Felise continues to push the cart down the aisle in front of us.

"Since when do you and Felise have a secret handshake?" Melanie asks. She's looking annoyed at Felise, who is thankfully out of earshot.

"I don't know," I answer honestly. I had no idea that I had all that hand-eye coordination in me!

"How come you didn't teach it to me?" Melanie asks. She sounds mad at me.

"Hold on a second," I say, kind of surprised that she's so upset. "You have special handshakes with your teammates. You never taught any of those to *me*."

"That's different," she says.

"Why?" I ask. "Because you're all on a team together?" Now *I'm* feeling a little mad. I can't believe we're having an argument in the condiment aisle, by jars of mayonnaise and mustard. "It makes me feel left out when you and Cassandra have your own handshake, but I also know that a person can have more than one good friend." The problem is, I haven't had more than one good friend other than Melanie, and she knows it. "Felise can show you the handshake and then we can all do it. Together."

"Forget it. It's not a big deal." Melanie says this in a way that lets me know it's a very big deal. It's what Mom calls passive-aggressive behavior. It's something that my grandmother on my dad's side spends a lot of time doing when she visits, or so Mom says. I try to stay out of it. "You've been spending an awful lot of time with Felise lately."

"Yeah. And you've been spending a lot of time with your soccer team," I say.

"I have to! We have practice and games and team dinners." Melanie's voice is high and strained.

"And that's all good," I say. "But even when you don't have that stuff, it feels like you want to hang out with them more than you want to hang out with me."

"That's not true," she says, but her eyes move to the floor. I know there isn't anything fascinating on the linoleum underneath our sneakers.

"It's kind of true," I say with a shrug. "I think it's cool you have soccer, and everyone on the team was really nice when we all had ice pops."

"Yeah, it was so weird that truck stopped by, right when the game was over." Melanie shakes her head, then meets my eyes again. "I didn't know you felt left out. Why didn't you say anything?"

"We've both been busy," I lie. Playing the triangle doesn't take up as much of my time as soccer does for her.

"I'm never too busy for you," Melanie says.

"Same goes for me," I say. We smile at each other. We don't need a dumb handshake to know what our friendship is all about.

I walk down toward the end of the aisle and look for Felise. "Where did she go?"

"I don't know," Melanie says, walking beside me. "Now that you mention it, when did we become friends with Felise? I can't remember."

She's the first person to question where Felise came from. I can't tell if that's a good thing or a bad thing.

"It feels like she came into our lives only yesterday," I say. I feel only a little guilty that I'm not straight up lying to my oldest friend. We look down a few more aisles until we find Felise standing in checkout line number seven.

"Yoo-hoo! Over here," Felise says, waving us over. "I

think we have all that we need." I look at the cart. It's full of lots of groceries that are way out of my league, money-wise.

"What's the frozen shrimp for?" I ask. All this outrageous food can't possibly be for a school bake sale.

"I learned an exquisite recipe for seafood empanadas during my time in Argentina," Felise says. "You will *adore* them!" She takes my hands in hers before placing them on the cart handle. "Now get in line and we can be on our merry way."

"We can't afford all this!"

But she doesn't seem to care. She just pushes me all the way to the credit card machine in front of the cashier. I'm about to excuse myself and deal with the embarrassment of having to put things back when an alarm rings out.

I duck down, thinking something dangerous is happening. Maybe there's a fire! Until I hear applause. Confetti falls down on me. I stand up and see a lot of the employees clapping. An employee with a ShopTilYouDrop name tag that says CHET and GENERAL MANAGER on it rushes toward me while holding a giant piece of cardboard paper. Chet is followed by Yolanda Jones, the local news reporter on channel 7 that we watch in the evening. A camera crew is with her and follows her every move.

"We are here at ShopTilYouDrop in the Providential Hills Pavilion," Yolanda says into her microphone as she gets closer to me. "Celebrating the store's one millionth customer. We have a very surprised winner here. Do we have your permission to film you?" Yolanda asks me.

"Uh, yes?" I say, confetti still landing on my shoulders and hair. I can't tell where it's actually coming from.

"What's your name?" Yolanda asks. She's even more beautiful in person than she is on TV, which doesn't make sense.

"Lila," I say and look over my shoulder at my friends. Melanie's lower jaw looks like it's about to reach her belly button. Felise claps for me, tears in her eyes, smiling the way a parent would when their kid wins the national spelling bee.

"Well, Lila, this is your lucky day!" Yolanda continues. I glance back at the camera. My mouth feels dry and my cheeks get hot. I think about all the people who might be watching me on the evening news. I wish I'd brushed my hair better this morning or worn a shirt that didn't have Snoopy on it. (My favorite Charles M. Schulz character is Marcie, but I don't have a shirt with her on it. Yet.)

"The ShopTilYouDrop company, the one place for all your shopping needs," Yolanda recites cheerfully, "and also a corporate sponsor of channel seven. They want to show their appreciation for the community and all who shop at their stores. Here we have general manager Carl Bensen to present you with a special prize."

The general manager wedges himself between Yolanda and me.

"It's Chet," the manager says into Yolanda's microphone.

"Potato, po-tah-to, Chet. People mispronounce my name all the time." Yolanda says this with a sparkling smile, even though it's kind of rude. I get her, though. People mispronounce my name a lot too. I should do what Chet did and correct someone if they say my name wrong.

"On behalf of the ShopTilYouDrop family, we would like to award you"—Chet begins, staring straight into the camera instead of talking to me. He looks as nervous as I do and a rash is breaking out on his neck—"with a lifetime supply of chocolate pudding, a lawn mower, and all the groceries in your cart today."

That's why Felise was so casual about what she plopped into our cart!

"And what else, Chet?" Yolanda asks. Her smile is still in place, but I can hear her grinding her teeth.

"Oh! Sorry!" Chet hurriedly flips over the giant piece of cardboard he's carrying. It's a giant check for five thousand dollars!

"Wow, that is quite a sum of money for a young person," Yolanda says, putting the microphone in my face. "What do you plan on doing with it?"

My mind goes blank. I forget where I am and how I got here. I only focus on how much money they're giving me and how many people might be watching and expecting me to laugh or cry or pass out. Then I remember everyone in band who is counting on me. They're the reason this whole thing started in the first place!

"I . . . I'm going to donate it to my school's music program," I say. I hear aaahs all around me, which makes me blush even more. It doesn't seem fair that as a society we need to give people giant checks on television in order to fund educational programs for young people, but I don't make the rules.

I feel someone put their arm around my shoulder. Felise grins right into the camera.

"If all you generous so-and-sos out there would like to support young people in their pursuit of mastering the arts, we'll be holding a bake sale at Providential Hills Middle School this weekend. For more info, check out lilaistheluckiest.com. Come one, come all!"

Since when do I have a website?

"No child should have to squelch the song that springs like a babbling brook in their heart." She bats her eyelashes at that last part. I have no doubt the camera loves it.

Chapter Nine

"Hey, Lila! You were great on TV last night," Cassandra says when Felise and I exit the school.

There's been a lot of that today. I can't lie, it felt *really, really* awesome for kids at school to notice me. Not that I want to be famous or popular or anything—that seems like a lot of work—but I enjoy feeling like a valued part of the middle school community. Everybody cheered for me this morning in homeroom and Ms. Zeller even said how proud she was of my generous gift to the school. The best part was Felise wasn't making them do any of that. I could tell they really meant it. To be honest, Felise didn't even say much in our classes today, not even when Mr. Hernandez played "For She's a Jolly Good Fellow" on the piano and everyone in band joined in serenading me.

"Let's walk a different way home," Felise says, taking a right where I'd normally take a left.

"How come?" I ask. As soon as the question leaves my mouth, she gives me a *surely you can't be serious* look. It's our third day together and she hasn't steered me wrong yet. "Forgive me. Lead the way, O fortuitous one."

"Fortuitous one! Brava." Felise actually seems impressed with my poking fun at the way she talks. "I thought we might investigate the park. On a whim, you might say."

"Do you ever *not* follow your whims?" I ask it jokingly, but kind of marvel at how she seems to do whatever she wants. Most people without magic or the power of luck aren't always able to do that.

"I wish I could follow all my wants and desires," Felise says, now a little less chipper. "I'd like to give luck to as many people as I possibly can. There are those who could really use my services."

"I wish you could too," I say. I'm starting to feel a bit guilty. I should be doing more to help others this week, but I suppose we both have our limits. We keep walking about half a mile until we reach the public park. There are a lot of people surrounding the playground basketball courts. I can read the sign hanging above the risers: BATTLE OF THE BUCKETS.

"We are right on schedule!" Felise guides me to a table on a grassy area. There are a few attendants seated there, asking people for their names.

"What are we doing here?" I ask Felise. There are a lot of athletic adults wearing serious basketball gear. I wish I could pull off a sweatband around my forehead as a fashion statement. Felise ignores me and steps to the front of the check-in line.

"Yes, my friend is here for the shooting contest," she says to one of the attendants manning the table.

"I'm what?!" I yelp. "I'm not good at basketball! I mean, I shoot around with my family, but I don't play on a team or anything." Felise doesn't seem to care about my concerns.

"Name?" the volunteer asks.

"Moradi," Felise says. The volunteer flips through the pages to look for my name.

"I don't see it here," the volunteer says. I peek to take a look in the M section. I don't see my name either.

"Guess we better be going, then," I say, backing away from the table only to have Felise grip me by my arm. The volunteer looks past us to help the next competitor. Felise doesn't give up.

"Would you mind checking your list one more time, please?" Felise asks. The volunteer looks annoyed but stares down at the paper again.

"Huh," the volunteer says. "Must have missed it. Here's your number." She passes me a race bib with the number seven on it. "You'll be on court four."

"Thank you!" Felise says, wrapping her arm around me and turning me toward the court we've been told to go to.

"Felise, I'm not that good." I size up the much taller competitors around me. It looks like I'm the youngest person participating in the contest. "There are grown-ups and high schoolers here!"

"Last night you told me you enjoy basketball," she says.

"Yes, to watch and play for fun! But this is, like, serious!" I watch a DJ in a gold tracksuit speak into a microphone. The radio banner hanging on the chain link fence reads GROOVIN' 107.7. I don't listen to the radio much, but it's not a station I've ever heard of. And it's definitely not the one that Parisa called into to win tickets to last year's Pop Fest 3000.

"All right, hoopers, how are you feeling?" the DJ says. The big crowd on the bleachers cheers, but I guess it isn't up to the DJ's standards. "I don't think you *he-e-eard me*! Hoopers, how are you all feeling?!"

"FANTASTIC!" Felise shouts right in my ear. The crowd cheers loudly enough that the DJ seems satisfied.

"Our next shootaround of the day is the buzzer beater contest," the DJ says. "So would the contestants please make your way to the center of the court." I turn to leave, but my legs won't let me. Felise isn't even touching me, but I know her magic is responsible.

"Let's not dillydally," Felise says, holding a Providential Hills Middle School jersey in her hands with the number seven on it. She puts it over my head. The jersey drapes over me and ends past my knees. I'm swimming in it.

She pins the racer bib on my back. "Go out there and show them your stuff!"

"I don't have stuff!" I exclaim, but it's too late. My legs are moving me out to half-court, even though my nervous system didn't tell them to do that! They stop once I get in line between two people who are both about a foot and a half taller than I am.

"This isn't the juniors contest," the contestant on my right says. "You sure you're in the right place, kid?"

"Yes," I say with a sigh. Felise brought me here for a reason—and even if she didn't, she's not giving me much of a choice. I'll have to talk to her about that. It's not good to make people do things they don't want to do.

"Are you all ready?" the DJ asks. "Let's remind everybody what this group is playing for today. If you can make one shot from half-court, you'll win two tickets to this year's Pop Fest 3000. If you can make two shots, you'll win a deluxe drum set. And, if you've *really* got the magic touch and can make shot number three, you can bank *five thousand dollars*, courtesy of yours truly and all the gang at Groovin' 107.7."

There's no way I'm going to make even one basket, but if I did, I wonder who I'd take to the concert. Melanie would be my first choice, but Parisa would be mad at me if I didn't take her. Then again, she didn't take *me* when she won tickets. Well, it's probably for the best that I'm not going to make a shot anyway.

"So, no pressure," the DJ continues. "Those of you watching from the sidelines, you're going to want to capture the greatness on your phones. Don't forget to tag Groovin' 107.7 in all your clips. You never know who might have what it takes to make the winning basket."

I try to remember everything I've learned from gym class and my parents. Sometimes when I finish my homework, they'll let me watch games with them on weeknights, but I have to go to bed right after the fourth quarter, even if the game goes into overtime. Summer's better because that's when the WNBA season is underway and I don't have to worry about homework, but sometimes I can't find those games on TV. Women's sports always get shortchanged. Anyway, I know to square my feet up to the basket, one foot in front of the other. I know to bend my knees. I know how to hold the ball with a little space between it and my palm. And I know that once I release the ball, I should leave my arm up and follow through. I don't know *what* that's supposed to do, but it looks sweet.

"Let's have our first contestant come up and give it a try," the DJ says.

"It's in the bag," the contestant to my right exclaims and waves their muscular arms to the crowd to make some noise. The ref at half-court hands my competition the ball. The DJ lets the crowd know that it must be shot before the twenty seconds on the shot clock is up. Countdown music plays, the contestant dribbles the ball a few times, squares up, hurls the ball in the air, and hits the rim with a giant clang.

"Oh, that's too bad," the DJ says. "Let's give it up for contestant number one." Contestant number one—the person who asked if I was in the wrong contest—stomps off the court. "Contestant number two, come on down!"

The game continues and participants of different genders, races, and ages all go up to shoot their shots. All of them are tall, athletic, and look like they have a good chance of making it. All of them either airball, missing the basket by a mile, or hit the rim and backboard.

"And our last contestant, lucky number seven," the DJ says. I cringe. As soon as I walk out to half-court, I hear the crowd laugh and make loud bets about how badly I'm going to miss. The ref hands me the ball.

"Thank you," I say and stare at the ball in my hands.

"You know the drill," the DJ says. He plays an old hip-hop song where the artist says he wishes he was a little bit taller and he wishes he was a baller. Those are lyrics I can relate to in this moment. I get in position and dribble, listening to the crowd count down from ten. I bend my knees, then launch the ball in the air with all my might. The net swishes when the ball goes through the hoop.

"WE HAVE A WINNER!" the DJ cries. Then he plays the song even louder. The crowd goes wild! I turn my head to look for Felise. She gives me a *wow, how about that* expression, but when she smirks right after, I know I've had some help. "Let's see if she can make it two in a row."

The ref hands me the ball again, wishing me good luck this time. I look over at the crowd and many of them have their phones pointed at me. I do exactly what I did for the last shot. I figure even if Felise is helping me, I might as well give it a real try and make it look legitimate. I dribble away from half-court, then run and dribble back to the spot I'm supposed to shoot from. I bend my knees and release the ball as I hop forward. This time it hits the window of the backboard but miraculously drops in the bucket.

"WHOA! TWO FOR TWO!" the DJ shouts into the microphone and the crowd roars with astonishment. "Now let's see if she can do it blindfolded!"

The ref hands me the ball, then puts a blindfold on me and asks if I can see anything. I can't. There's no way anybody could make this shot, even if they had all the luck in the world on their side. I don't dribble the ball, because I'd probably lose it as soon as I let go.

The DJ plays another song and the crowd counts down. I place the ball in my dominant hand, then fire it in a hook shot. Before I can take off my blindfold, I hear the crowd go absolutely haywire.

I guess that means my shot went in!

Chapter Ten

"Would Lila Moradi please come to Principal Li's office?" a voice on the school PA system says during homeroom.

What did I do? Since winning the shooting contest a day ago, life has gotten so busy. I haven't had *time* to do anything that would get me into trouble.

The videos people took on their phones of my winning baskets have gone viral, especially the one where I was wearing a blindfold. My family got a lot of calls from news outlets and I even did an interview with ESPN. There's also a sports drink company called I Can't Believe It's Not Juice that saw the footage and wants to do a commercial with me! I don't even drink their product because it looks like toxic sludge in a bottle. But, hey, I can get down with electrolytes if they pay for the music program to stick around for years to come. And my college tuition to boot!

"Maybe you got another endorsement deal," Melanie whispers to me with excitement. I stand up and Felise does the same.

"Where are you going, Felise?" Ms. Zeller asks.

"I am accompanying Lila," Felise says. "Naturally."

"Only Lila was called to Principal Li's office," Ms. Zeller says. Felise sits back down at her desk. Other than going to the restroom, it's the first time she hasn't been near me all week. I exit the classroom and walk down the hallway and around the corner to Principal Li's office.

I knock on the door and hear Principal Li tell me to come in.

She stands up from behind her desk. She looks really excited to see me, which hasn't ever happened before. Someone is sitting in the armchair in front of her, but I can only see their hand on the armrest.

"Lila! Just the student we wanted to see," Mrs. Li says.

"We have a special visitor who is eager to meet you."

The mysterious visitor stands up, wearing a black over-coat with a black necktie around his thick neck. The hand on the armrest belongs to Mr. Mammonton—the man who dropped Felise's key at the bank. I feel a little sick and dizzy but try not to show it.

"It's a pleasure to finally meet you, Ms. Moradi," Mr. Mammonton says, holding his hand out to me. He's doing his best to smile, or at least I think that's what he's trying to do. The expression on his face looks like he smells something awful and is pretending he hasn't. In any case, he's not scowling like he did at the bank when he ran into me.

"Hi," I say and shake his hand. We both let go as fast as we can. Principal Li gestures for me to have a seat in the armchair next to Mr. Mammonton's. I stay standing until Mr. Mammonton sits down again. When he does, I plop down in my chair, wishing it was farther away from his.

"Mr. Mammonton's interested in investing in our school's extracurricular programs," Principal Li says. She waves her hand over a glass bowl, offering me a candy.

I'm pretty sure she doesn't do this when other students come in to see her. "And it's all because of you."

If I'm responsible for getting a really rich guy to give the school money, I guess I'm entitled to a fun-size candy bar, even if it is Mounds. Yuck.

"Yes," Mr. Mammonton says in a calm tone. "Particularly your music program."

"Mr. Mammonton saw the news coverage of you at the ShopTilYouDrop giveaway and the basketball contest," Principal Li explains. "He was so impressed with your willingness to donate your prize money to the school. He wants to meet with students like you who show promise."

"Quite," Mr. Mammonton says. "How *fortunate* you've been this week."

I try to play it casual and relaxed, like I don't know that he knows what we both know. You know?

"And," Principal Li blurts out before I can answer, "Mr. Mammonton is inviting you, your homeroom, and the band club to his facilities tomorrow for a behind-the-scenes tour! Isn't that exciting?"

No, it isn't, Principal Li! It fills me with dread

and remorse and anxiety! (All words I learned from *The Woodchuck Brigade*. It was entertaining and educational. I'm hoping there will be a reboot one day.)

"Oh," I say instead. "That's nice of you. Kind of out of the blue, though." Principal Li widens her eyes at me to let me know I've said the wrong thing.

"It isn't every day one hears about such a selfless student," Mr. Mammonton says. I doubt he generally pays so much attention to student achievements.

"I don't know if I can visit the offices tomorrow," I say. "What with the bake sale coming up. My friends and I have a lot to prepare."

"I can guarantee, with my financial assistance, you won't need to bother yourself with a bake sale," Mr. Mammonton says. He turns his nose up when he says that, but maybe his nose is always in that position. "By the by, I have some contacts at the Providential Hills Bank. The institution would be more than willing to collaborate with your school on any future fundraising efforts. You're familiar with their location, yes?"

He asks the question cheerfully enough, but his eyes are icy and his jaw tightens. He recognizes me from the bank. He knows I have his box. I should give it back to him. I mean, it was his!

But after looking up all his business dealings, I'd hate to think about what he could do with Felise's powers. I'd also hate to think about Felise not being around me anymore—and not because of all the magic stuff either. I'd miss her.

"Can't say that I am," I say. I look at Principal Li to avoid Mr. Mammonton's stare. "I mean, I'm a kid. What would I do at a bank? It's so boring there." Now Principal Li's smile is completely gone, and that one vein in her forehead is poking out.

"I wouldn't characterize it as such," Mr. Mammonton says coolly. "You can bump into the most unassuming people there." My stomach could churn an incredible amount of butter right now. "Well, I'd better be going," he says, standing up again. "I do hope to see you tomorrow."

"We're thrilled to be invited, Mr. Mammonton." Principal Li says. She rushes to stand up and trips a little over her desk to shake his hand. "I'll print out some permission slips for the students to take home to their guardians tonight."

Permission slips! If my parents don't sign, I don't have to go!

"It's been a pleasure, Lila," Mr. Mammonton says. "And if for some reason you aren't able to make it, I'd be more than happy to pay you a visit at your home. I'd love to meet your parents and congratulate them on raising such a bright young student."

Nothing in his voice changes, but I know a threat when I hear one. He knows who I am, where I live, and that I have his key. I know he's powerful, and from what I've read about him, he has a history of doing a lot of bad things to get his way.

"I'll see you tomorrow," I say. I don't want him messing with my family.

❁❁❁

"What did Principal Li want?" Melanie asks me before Felise and I head into band.

"Nothing," I say.

I haven't wanted to explain the truth about Mr. Mammonton to Felise. If she finds out that I wasn't the key's original owner, she might get mad or decide to leave early.

"Pretty great about the last-minute field trip, huh?" Melanie asks. She waves a permission slip in front of my face. "I hear they make all kinds of strange tech at Mammonton Industries. Top secret hush-hush gadgets!"

I'm glad someone is excited to go. Other than Principal Li anyway.

"Are you feeling unwell, Lila?" Felise asks me. I really do have to work on the whole poker face thing.

"A little," I say. Felise frowns and puts her palm against my forehead, checking for a fever.

"Your temperature is normal for a human being," Felise says. "I don't understand. Illness never happens on my watch."

Melanie doesn't even give Felise a funny look. I guess she's gotten used to Felise saying weird things over the past five days.

"I'm fine," I lie, which makes me feel worse. Both Felise and Melanie look at me like they don't believe me. "I'm just a little overwhelmed with all the attention and everything." Which is true, but I don't tell them why I'm really upset.

"Listen, if you want me to take your place in that

commercial, I'm game." Melanie says this with a laugh but it's the fake kind. I try to smile, but I think she can tell her joke doesn't help lighten my mood. I don't want her or Felise to worry. "I better get to practice. You sure you're okay?"

"Yeah. I'll see you tomorrow," I say. Melanie waves bye to both of us and Felise follows me into Mr. Hernandez's class. A bunch of the band kids, including Carolina and Veronica, are surrounding the new deluxe drum set.

"It was delivered this afternoon," Mr. Hernandez tells me. "You really didn't have to donate this. You've given so much already."

"It's no big deal," I say with a shrug. I didn't earn it. My hook shot isn't that good without magical assistance.

"Would you excuse us for a moment, Mr. Hernandez?" Felise asks my teacher and drags me to our seats. Then she turns and looks at me intensely. "Have I done something wrong?"

"What?" I ask.

"You don't seem yourself," Felise says. "Not since this morning." I'm not sure if super-empathy is a part of her powers, but she's sensing something's wrong. "And Mr. Hernandez is right. You have given quite a lot. Most people I've joined forces with in the past haven't given anywhere near as much as you have. They only think about how to advance their own needs. It is a *very* big deal that you've donated the drum set."

"You're the very big deal," I respond a little defensively. "The only reason that drum set is here is because of you. When you leave, I'm going to be back to how I was."

Felise is about to say something when she's interrupted by Jimmy's entrance.

"Whoa!" Jimmy just stands in the doorway, staring at the drum set. The other kids back away from it as he walks into the room so he can get a good look. "Where did this come from?"

"Lila won it," Carolina says with a soft smile. "Isn't it incredible?"

Jimmy approaches the drums slowly. He puts his fingers on the cymbal, then circles the black-and-red set. It has a green four-leaf clover on the biggest drum. Jimmy carefully picks up the drumsticks from the holster attached to the set.

"If Lila won it, what is it doing here?" he asks, still captivated. He's clutching the drumsticks in his fist so tight. The students and Mr. Hernandez pay me attention and wait for me to answer.

"Well, if Jimmy's parents don't let him play the drums at home," I say, "or if any other kid wants to learn to play, I thought we should have a set here. For everybody." Jimmy looks up at me, still holding the drumsticks. He moves closer to me.

"Seriously?" he asks. "I mean, if I won it I'd probably keep it all to myself."

To be fair, I am keeping the lifetime supply of chocolate pudding and the concert tickets. I'm not *that* selfless. I'm still not sure what to do with the lawn mower, but I'll cross that bridge when I get to it.

"I like that music brings people together," I say. "I'm not great at it, but you all let me play with you anyway, and it's meant a lot to me. I figured it would also mean a lot to someone else who wants to play here if we keep band going." The room is silent. Even Felise doesn't chime in. I feel kind of embarrassed I said all that.

Jimmy stands in front of me and holds out the drumsticks.

"You've got to be the first to play them," he says. Then he smiles so wide, I can't help but do the same. I take the drumsticks from him and the classroom cheers me on. I sit behind the drums and Jimmy coaches me. The rest of the afternoon we all laugh and take turns playing, making so much noise and having a blast even when we're not that good. Well, except for Felise. She busts out a solo so epic, Mr. Hernandez asks if she can give him some pointers.

I feel better about things when I'm in the room, but when it's time to go, I find I don't want to leave. Leaving means I'm closer to tomorrow's visit to Mammonton Industries.

I don't know what Mr. Mammonton has in store, but I'm not going to let him take Felise away.

Chapter Eleven

I forget to put the cap on the blender. Chunks of chopped walnuts fly out of the top of the mixer and ricochet off the kitchen sink and coffee machine. I turn it off, wishing we'd decided to make brownies from a box for the bake sale. Baklava was a little too ambitious.

"Are you sure you don't want my *real* assistance?" Felise asks, swirling her pointer finger in the air. I told her that if we were going to bake together, I didn't want her to use her powers. She still doesn't understand why, and now that I'm looking at the mess I've made on the kitchen island, I'm not sure I understand either.

"No. I have to get used to doing things on my own," I say, blowing a strand of hair out of my face. Felise is wearing an apron that doesn't have a smidge of phyllo dough or honey on it.

"So you've said." Felise purses her lips and raises an eyebrow.

"You can help me clean up, though," I say as I rip off a paper towel to pick some nuts off the floor. Some of them float in the air before I can get to them. "Not that kind of help!" The nut bits drop and crumble, becoming even smaller than before.

I hear her footsteps walk away. I figure I'm on my own. She doesn't seem like the type to stoop down or get her hands dirty. Or so I thought until she stands over me, holding a broom and dustpan.

"This seems more efficient," she says. She hands me the dustpan. I hold it while she sweeps nuts my way. "It's been quite some time since I've had baklava, but is it meant to have a smoky flavor?"

"No. Why?"

"If I'm not mistaken, I think that's smoke coming out of the oven."

I turn around to look and sure enough some smoke is inching out of the top.

"Shoot!" I say. I rush to the oven to turn it off. When I open the door, smoke billows out and I start to cough.

"Is everything all right?" I hear Mom say behind me. Before I can utter a word, she has a fire extinguisher in hand and pointed at the oven in case something is on fire.

"You certainly are prepared, Mrs. Moradi," Felise says.

"Too prepared," I grumble. Mom promised she was going to let Felise and me bake by ourselves, but deep down I'm kind of glad she's here to help. I should know she wouldn't leave me totally unsupervised. Mom sets the fire extinguisher down and puts on some oven mitts. She pulls out a tray of baklava that's charcoal black and reeks of ash.

"Oh dear," Felise says, peeking over Mom's shoulder. "Perhaps we could repurpose them for something else?"

"Like what?" I ask, worried about how long making a new batch is going to take. At this rate, I'll be up all night.

"They could serve as some sort of garnish?" Felise suggests.

"For roadkill?!" I exclaim. I almost start to cry, then think about how sweet Felise is trying to be about it and laugh instead. All three of us laugh, Mom cracking up while she takes the tray to the trash.

"What's so funny?" Parisa asks as she strolls into the kitchen wearing her pajamas. She waves away the smoke still in the air. Dad follows her from the den, where he was finishing up some work on his computer.

"I made the mistake of trying to make baklava," I say. "I guess I'm better off making the brownies from a box."

"What if we all helped?" Mom asks.

"An inspired idea," Felise says, clapping her hands until she sees my reaction. "Helping in the typical mundane human way, of course."

"How else would we help?" Parisa asks with a chuckle. "The outer space alien way?"

"They've made contact here again?" Felise asks. "I thought they weren't due for another thousand years after the Area 51 disaster." Everybody looks at her for a moment, trying to make sense of what she's said. Felise must then realize that Parisa wasn't being serious and maybe she's said some things we weren't meant to know. "I jest!" She clears her throat, then thankfully Mom takes the lead.

"It looks like you've already got some nuts chopped up, which is great," Mom says. "And there's plenty of dough. How about your father and I take care of the blender and you, Felise, and Parisa lay out the dough on another tray?"

I expect Parisa to complain or say how she can't help out because she has some last-minute championship dodgeball tournament to go to. Instead, she walks to the sink and starts to wash her hands.

"You're staying?" I ask, with a mixture of confusion and hope.

She finishes washing her hands. "Of course," Parisa says, putting on an apron. "I don't know how to make baklava and I'd like to learn. My baking skills are so-so, but I figure practice makes better." She dries her hands and pulls another baking tray out of a drawer.

"Doesn't practice make perfect?" I ask as I join her at

the kitchen island. She places the empty tray down and smiles at me.

"Nobody's perfect," Parisa says. She sounds like she actually means it! I wonder if Felise has put some kind of spell on her? Felise lets me know she hasn't by hugging both of us.

"A sisterly moment!" Felise squeals. "I love to see one happen organically."

"Lila, tell your friend to stop squeezing the life out of me," Parisa says. Felise lets go, apparently not realizing her own strength.

"Apologies, I get excited over familial bonding," she says. She's still wedged between us.

"Speaking of familial bonding," Parisa says, tying her apron straps behind her. "How about a game of Life after we finish in here?"

Yup, Parisa is still Parisa all right.

"I am thoroughly exhausted," Felise says, falling down face-first on my bed. "I won't complain if I never see another piece of baklava again."

"I hope they're a hit," I say. We tasted some before

brushing our teeth and the pastry was delicious. I didn't win the game of Life we all played after baking, since Felise respected my wishes and didn't use her abilities. But Mom won and I felt pretty good about that. Parisa still had trouble with losing, but she didn't ask to play more games or have the same meltdown she did a few days ago.

Felise rolls over to look at me. "How do any of you do anything without the power of luck on your side?" she asks as she gets under my duvet. It used to bother me that she took my bed, but now I think it's been fun to share a room with her.

"I guess I'll find out again in two days," I say, trying not to sound sad.

"I'm not so sure about that," Felise says. For once, her sleeping eye mask doesn't appear out of thin air. "From what I can tell over the course of our time together, you have had a lot of luck on your side before I even arrived."

"How do you figure?" I lie down on my futon, which has grown weirdly comfier over time. If Felise could stay longer, I'd actually be okay with sleeping on the futon for a while more.

Felise stares at the ceiling, thinking for a moment before explaining what she means.

"You have a wonderful family that enjoys spending time with you," Felise says. "Your father writes notes for you in your lunch box. Your mother helps you when you burn pastry beyond recognition. Even Parisa can be a delight, in her surly teenage way. When she's not involved in some sort of competition."

"When is she *not* competing?" I say with a snort. Felise lies on her side, her chin in her hand, and speaks directly to me.

"Your friend Melanie is very sweet and senses when you're upset. You are able to communicate easily with her. Your classmates in band are happy to play music with you. I think if you got to know them better, they'd want to 'hang out' with you outside school. You're clearly smart; you haven't needed my help at all with your schoolwork. Aside from that one silly math problem, but who cares when two trains are going to get to Albuquerque if they leave from the same station at different rates of speed anyhow?"

Yeah, I definitely didn't get the right answer to that

question, but Ms. Zeller said it was for extra credit and wouldn't impact our grade.

"You have a lovely home, which is tastefully decorated by the way," Felise continues. "You have food, all of it delicious. You have clothes. Granted, you don't feel they're very hip, but I'd say you have your own unique sense of style. And you have a good heart, Lila, donating your winnings to those who need it. I suspect you have a bright future ahead of you. Some people don't get that lucky."

She's right. I guess I only paid attention to what I was missing before Felise came, but I do have a lot of luck in my life, even if I don't always notice it. I'm going to make sure I notice a lot more from now on.

"I'm still going to miss you," I admit.

"I know," Felise says fluffing her hair for show. "Once people get a hold of my power, they find it difficult to see me go. But as I said, you have lots of luck already. I don't think you'll miss my abilities too often."

"No, it's not that," I say. She raises her eyebrows in confusion. "You were always here to listen to me and hang out with. It was nice having someone in my corner.

I hope you had some fun this week too. I know it's probably been dorky hanging out with a middle schooler compared to all the other interesting people you've helped."

Felise has a look I can't figure out. Her eyes get a little watery, and she seems stumped about how to respond.

"I have had a *wonderful* time," she says softly. She says it in a way that makes my heart hurt, but I don't know why. Before any tears spill, however, she snaps out of it and switches back to her bubbly, fancy self. "Don't think I've forgotten about our interrupted exchange at band rehearsal. You said that when I leave, your life will go back to how it was. What was your life like before I arrived?"

I didn't get sponsorship deals from beverage companies or have birds greet me with a song when I woke up.

"Before you came, I felt like I didn't have a *thing*," I say quietly, thinking how dumb it sounds when I speak it aloud.

"Forgive me, but a *thing*? Could you elucidate?"

"I could if I knew what elucidate meant."

"Ah. What do you mean by a *thing*?" Felise says with a grin, making an effort to speak like an average eleven-year-old kid.

"Melanie has soccer and she loves it. Carolina is incredible at piano. Parisa is good at *everything*. It feels like everyone at school has a place they belong to, or a passion for a class or club. I joined band and everyone is nice and I like it okay, but it's not something I feel like I really want to spend a lot of time on."

"I wondered why you didn't have much zeal for the triangle," Felise says with a nod. "Not to be condescending, but you do realize that at your age you don't need to have everything figured out, yes? I can tell you that for me, being eleven has been fascinating but also tremendously challenging."

"It has?" I wouldn't think someone who's seen as much as she's seen and has the powers she does would find anything challenging.

"Oh yes! All this energy I have inside, figuring out social hierarchies and who deserves my friendship and who doesn't, a packed schedule full of classes and homework. I've seen most of the world and all that it has to offer, and yet I still have no idea what is in that mystery meat! It has been bothering me for days!" I giggle a little at that. I don't know what's in it either. I have a feeling that's probably for the best. "I would also argue that you do have interests that could qualify as a *thing*."

"Like what?"

Felise points to the posters, comic strips, and drawings of animated shows and movies on the walls around my room.

"You have an affinity for art," Felise says, tilting her head in the direction of a small drawing I did of *The Woodchuck Brigade* hanging by my desk. "Did you create that?"

"Well, yeah, but it's not that great," I murmur. I drew a lot this past summer when Melanie was at soccer camp.

"No. It is not great. It's sublime! May I?" Felise twirls her finger in the air. I nod and as soon as I do, my drawing floats from the desk to her hands. She regards it up close for a moment before she turns it around to show me.

"It's not original art," I say, my face feeling hot. "I mean, those characters aren't mine. I was just goofing around."

"From this illustration, it is evident you have the beginnings of a gift," Felise says. "Did you enjoy working on this?"

"I do love animation and comics," I admit. "But I wouldn't show anyone at school my stuff. Especially not anything to do with *The Woodchuck Brigade*. It's a kids' show that nobody watches anymore. It'd be too embarrassing."

"Would it be?" Felise asks. And I realize then that she doesn't really get embarrassed. At least not that I've seen. "I don't believe there's anything shameful about things that don't harm anyone and provide us and others joy. The real shame would be in *not* pursuing one's interests. In trying to be like everyone else, no?" She lets go of the drawing. It floats in my direction and lands on my blanket.

I look at my work and see the flaws, but I also like that I've given the characters some life in their eyes. I remember it took me a long time to figure out how to do that, but I didn't mind because I was really focused on what I was doing.

"Want to see my comic book collection?" I ask. I'm testing the waters with someone my age, even if Felise isn't technically my age.

"Absolutely I do!" Felise sits up in bed. She looks genuinely interested as I pull out my boxes of bagged and boarded comics from under the bedframe, along with some of my favorite graphic novels.

We spend the next hour talking, Felise asking me questions like what a director of animation does and whatever happened in the end of a newspaper comic strip called *Flash Gordon*. I'm not familiar, but she says I simply must research it for her. I tell her about my favorite voice actors like Mel Blanc, Cree Summer, Kevin Conroy, and Tara Strong. I'd keep going, but I let out a yawn.

"Excuse me," I say, forgetting to cover my mouth with my hand.

"It's quite all right. Perhaps we had better retire for the evening." Felise waves her hand and my entire collection zips back into their boxes. She doesn't use her powers to push the boxes under the bed, though. Instead, she has them glide across the floor and then float up to the top tier of my desk. "There! Now you can have your treasure trove more readily available and not hidden away."

I want to tell her that I hid my comics away because should anyone ever break in, I don't want them to take issue number one of *The Woodchuck Brigade*. (Comics appreciate in value over time.) Then I think of how silly that would sound and lay my head down on my pillow.

"Thanks for today," I say. "For everything, really."

"You're very welcome, Lila joon," Felise says. "I'm so glad the key found you."

My heavy eyelids open wide after she says that. Because the key didn't find me. It was meant for someone else.

And he means to collect.

Chapter Twelve

"Yowza," Jimmy says, his echo bouncing off the walls in the lobby of the main Mammonton Industries building. It's huge and could fit about five professional basketball courts. The marble floor we stand on is spotless. Whoever designed this place sure likes steel and granite. The glass windows surrounding us are tall and tinted, and there's no decor or art except for a giant clock that hangs on the wall above the security desk. There isn't any other furniture either, like chairs to sit on while you wait or tables to have coffee at. I notice video cameras pointed down at us from the tall ceiling. It makes me feel like my classmates and I have entered a huge and fancy cage.

"It's like a modern art museum without any art," Melanie whispers to me.

"Everybody, stay close together," Principal Li says. She leads us closer to the front desk. Ms. Zeller and Mr. Hernandez are chaperoning too, but they don't seem as excited as Principal Li is to be here. I guess Ms. Zeller doesn't get excited about most things, but usually Mr. Hernandez tries to engage us on field trips and asks questions about what we notice or how we can apply it to something we've studied. From the look of things, he doesn't have a whole lot to work with here.

"It's freezing," Veronica says, wrapping her arms around herself.

"Perhaps it is part of the frosty theming," Felise observes. She doesn't seem impressed with the place. "I'm all for minimalism, but this is a bit stark."

"No way, Tony Stark's facilities are way cooler," Jimmy says.

"I'm sorry?" Felise asks.

"Don't worry about it," I mutter. I'm trying to pay attention to what Principal Li is saying to the guard behind the security desk.

"Good morning!" Principal Li says loudly and with enthusiasm, so all of us can hear. "We are visiting from Providential Hills Middle School."

The guard doesn't smile and he has dark circles under his eyes. Not exactly the warm welcome Principal Li was expecting.

But she tries again, this time her voice at a lower volume. "We've been invited by Mr. Mammonton. I was told that his personal assistant was going to give us a tour. A Mr. Winslow Barnett?"

"Uh-huh," the security guard says, not looking up right away from the computer. "Mr. Barnett will meet you on the other side of security check." He nods toward the doors to the left of him. "We don't allow anything other than your person and clothing past those doors during tours. No bags, personal items, phones, jewelry, nothing aside from a pacemaker."

"That's a bit severe," Carolina says. I think so too, but I don't say anything. I don't want any more attention on me here. Then again, from the look of those cameras pointed right at us, I'm sure Mr. Mammonton is already paying me plenty of attention.

The key around my neck suddenly feels a lot heavier. Who would be in charge of holding on to it during our visit? Felise told me the key should always be with me, but if it got into the wrong hands, wouldn't that be just as bad? I need to find a place to hide it.

"Ms. Zeller," I say. She turns around and nods. "May I use the restroom before we go in?"

"Yes, but be quick, please," Ms. Zeller says. "I'll wait for you." I dash over toward the wall that has a restroom sign. Bathrooms are the only place Felise doesn't follow me into unless we're brushing our teeth together. I look around the cold, gray, tiled room. Flushing the key isn't an option, and there aren't any windows for me to throw it out of and retrieve later. There's a potted green plant in the corner, the only bit of color in the place. I take off the necklace, crouch down to the floor, and dig a hole with my hand into the soil of the plant. Then I bury the key deep down at the base of the pot. I wash my hands, making sure there isn't any dirt underneath my fingernails. After the tour, I'll come back and dig the key out and nobody will be the wiser. I hope.

I leave the bathroom and Ms. Zeller is waiting for me.

The two of us join the rest of the group past a set of doors. There are two guards telling students to put their items on the conveyor belt to be x-rayed. Veronica walks underneath a body scan monitor. It's not unlike being at an airport, I guess, but we don't have to take off our shoes. And at the airport, they return stuff to passengers after they check it out.

Felise stands underneath the detector, where a security guard with a mustache is watching the monitor and looks confused.

"Could you go through again?" the security guard asks Felise.

"Is this absolutely necessary?" Felise asks, walking back inside the detector. She awaits further instruction. "I have to say, this is not the most hospitable way to greet guests."

The guard with the mustache looks at the monitor with a puzzled expression.

"Hey, Rita," he says to another guard with a tight bun and an even tighter grimace. "Could you take a look at this?"

Rita walks over from the conveyor belt to the monitor

and joins her co-worker in staring at Felise's scan.

"Huh," Rita says, looking back and forth from Felise to the monitor. "There's no body, Herbie. Machine must be on the fritz."

"It can't be," Herbie says, pointing at the screen. "What are all these tiny sparkly dots floating around?" I look at Felise, worried she's going to be found out. She might look like someone my age, but she's not exactly human. I'm not sure what she's actually made of. Felise rolls her eyes, waves her hand in Herbie and Rita's direction, and their expressions turn from bewildered to relaxed.

"The dots sure are pretty, though," Herbie mentions, a sleepy smile on his face.

"And they're so shiny," Rita says dreamily. "You're all set, young lady. Have a great day."

Felise walks toward Principal Li and most of the other students who have already been inspected.

"The rest of you can come on through," Herbie says. "Just leave your stuff on the conveyor belt. We'll get it to you safe and sound when you come back."

Carolina walks ahead of me, placing her backpack on the belt.

"This wasn't mentioned in our permission slips," Carolina says to me. "If I'd known they were keeping our stuff, I wouldn't have come."

"I guess whatever they make here is pretty important," I say. I left my backpack at school, so the only thing I have to give them is my *Woodchuck Brigade* button that I have pinned to my shoelace.

We're all shepherded through another set of doors. A giant Mammonton Industries logo hangs above an open office area with long desks, chairs, and computers. There are people wearing office clothes who walk and talk with one another as they pass us by. Some others sit at their desks, talking into headsets. There's absolutely no artwork on the walls and there isn't much color in the room either, but there is a buzz of activity. I hear people say things when they walk by us, like, "I need that data ASAP," or "The investors don't have time to wait."

"I'm stressed out just standing here," Melanie says, watching an employee talking into a phone about how they need some files yesterday or their job is toast.

"Hello, children," a man in a tight gray suit with a red

tie says as he races toward us. He's holding a Styrofoam coffee cup and reminds me a bit of Mr. Stuart from the bank, except he's a little older, a little taller, a little skinnier, and has a lot more energy. His teeth are blindingly white, and he shows us way too many of them. "I'm Mr. Barnett! It's so wonderful and surprisingly unexpected to have you here."

"Well, we are just so honored to have this opportunity," Principal Li says, before introducing herself to Mr. Barnett. He shakes her hand and speaks to her, but every so often his eyes make contact with mine. I look away, pretending I don't notice, but I have a feeling Mr. Mammonton told him to watch out for me.

"Mr. Mammonton is so sorry he couldn't show you around himself," Mr. Barnett says. His eyes are wide and his smile in place. His skin is really smooth, almost plastic looking. I wonder if he's had cosmetic surgery, so that his smile is permanently stuck that way? "Mr. Mammonton has many important meetings this morning. Meetings that I thought I would be a part of, considering I helped prepare for them over the course of several months . . . but never mind! What better way to spend my time than guiding middle school students on a field trip? If you'll just follow me, I'll show you where all the magic is made!" His smile is even wider than before as he turns around and quickly leads the way.

"You can't manufacture magic," Felise says with a huff. "What is he talking about?"

"It's just an expression," I explain. We all try to keep pace with the speedy Mr. Barnett.

"Still, how irresponsible to lie to children that way," Felise says. Mr. Barnett abruptly stops in front of a glass window that overlooks a factory floor. Down below, I can see full-size robots that have blocky heads full of gears and mechanical hands examining items on a conveyor belt. There are two human workers near the robots. At least I think they're human. I can't see much through the hazmat suits.

"Here is one of our assembly lines," Mr. Barnett says, "where we inspect, package, and distribute our products for the general public. I bet that some of your households have our goods in them right now."

"Like what?" Jimmy asks. I can't think I'd want anything that's made here in our home.

"Grow No More weed killer for gardens, Buzz Off spray for rodent and insect elimination, and Wipe Out bleach for laundry, to name a few," Mr. Barnett says with pride. Principal Li audibly murmurs in approval.

"That sure is a lot of poisonous material," Melanie says.

"Never heard of them," Jimmy says. Mr. Barnett ignores both of them.

"Didn't Grow No More get a lot of people sick about a year ago?" Carolina asks. Mr. Barnett is still smiling, but he's blinking a lot. "I saw it on the news and did a report on it for science class. Apparently there were traces of chemicals in the solution that hadn't been listed on the label."

"That was an unfortunate mischaracterization of our product by the media," Mr. Barnett explains. He has a strange amount of cheer in his voice for someone talking about something so serious. "Those who made the claims were adequately compensated in an out-of-court settlement. We haven't always found the press to be kind to us." He pauses for a moment. "I also don't recall that I was taking questions at this time. But I do appreciate your precociousness! Hold on to that curiosity for as long as you can."

"We will keep all questions under our hats until the end of the tour," Principal Li assures our guide.

"Splendid!" Mr. Barnett says. "Let's move on, shall we?" He turns and walks at an even faster clip.

"A bit high-strung, isn't he?" Felise asks wryly. I hear Ms. Zeller stifle a laugh as we all try to keep up with our highly caffeinated leader.

"Now, are you kiddos ready to see something *really* Gucci?" Mr. Barnett asks us from his seat at the head of a giant conference table. He's just finished showing us a film about Mammonton Industries and all the innovative things they do for the world. I haven't heard anyone say *Gucci* before with a straight face, but I think he's trying to relate to us. Carolina raises her hand. "Yeah, you're ready!"

"No, I wanted to ask a question," Carolina says, lowering her hand. "In the video, the narrator said your tech was changing things for the better, but aren't some of your automated machines responsible for taking jobs away from people?" Carolina is so smart. I wonder if she likes *The Woodchuck Brigade*? Even if she doesn't, it'd be cool to hang out with her more. Mr. Barnett takes a deep breath through his nose, but he doesn't remember to exhale right away and his eyes bug out a little.

"Could you tell us more about your work for the government?" Jimmy asks. "Like I heard you guys have an experimental program where you turn bunny rabbits into living recording devices, perfect for espionage. Is that true?"

The room is quiet for a moment. Mr. Barnett stares at Jimmy, his smile still frozen. It's the kind of smile that would belong to a creepy doll that no one wanted to buy, still stuck in the toy store waiting for someone to play with. It feels super tense. Jimmy, who was sitting on the edge of his seat waiting for an answer, starts to lean back. Then Mr. Barnett lets out a laugh. Only Principal Li joins him, but her laughter is uneasy.

"Where did you hear such an outlandish claim?" Mr. Barnett asks.

"The internet," Jimmy says quietly. Mr. Barnett stares at him without blinking.

"Well, I can assure you, that simply isn't true," Mr. Barnett says. "By the way, do you remember the website on which you found that fabricated information?" He pulls his phone out of his pocket and gets ready to type.

"No," Jimmy says.

Mr. Barnett puts his phone on the table in front of him.

"Well, no matter. I'll have our PR team search for that silly tidbit." He clears his throat. "In any case, all our work with the government is classified. Now, before I am interrupted again, I want to introduce you to a new friend of ours here at Mammonton Industries." He looks directly at me and I feel cold all over. "Young lady, would you like to help me with a demonstration?"

"It's okay. I'd rather not," I say, squirming in my seat.

"Of course, she would," Principal Li says.

"Come up here, please." Mr. Barnett stands and waves me over. Everyone stares at me, waiting for me to do something. It makes me nervous. I get up out of my chair and walk to the head of the table, standing next to Mr. Barnett. "I understand that you're the reason everyone is here today. Let's give Lila a big hand, everybody." Everyone claps but not like they did at school. I think it's because none of us have really had the greatest visit today. I also think it's strange that he knows my name, since none of us introduced ourselves to him. "Now, Lila, may I interest you in a coffee? Soda? Water?"

"I'm all set," I say.

"Water it is," Mr. Barnett says. "Hold out your hand, please. Hey, Polly?" Mr. Barnett shouts this toward the hall. "Can you bring Lila a water?"

I hear a whirring noise coming from outside the doorway. When I turn to look, a robotic parrot flies into the boardroom, carrying a plastic bottle of water in its giant mechanical claws. Everybody whispers as they watch the bird fly in. The parrot hovers closer to Mr. Barnett and me. Its beady eyes make mechanical sounds when they rotate.

"Polly," Mr. Barnett says. "This is Lila."

"Lila," the parrot says. Its voice sounds just like Mr. Barnett's.

"Polly, give the water to Lila," Mr. Barnett says. The

robotic bird hovers slowly toward my open hand. It lets go of the bottle with one of its talons, then passes it to me with the other one. When I hold it in my hand, Polly backs away, still in the air, waiting for the next command. "Now ask Polly a question using her name first."

The parrot clicks when it turns its head to the side, waiting for my question.

"Polly, want a cracker?" I ask. It's the only thing I can think of.

"I do not eat," Polly says, now in my voice. I hate it.

"Polly," Mr. Barnett says. "Would you land in the center of the table, please?"

The robotic bird does what it's told and hovers down in front of Mr. Hernandez, who looks freaked out.

"Polly," Mr. Barnett says. Polly's head clicks again when it looks in Mr. Barnett's direction. "What is the capital of East Timor?"

Polly clicks again, thinking about it for maybe half a second. "Dili," Polly says, mimicking Mr. Barnett's voice.

"Neat trick," Jimmy says. "But we have a device that answers questions like that at home."

Mr. Barnett narrows his eyes at Jimmy.

"Yes, but are those devices nearly sentient drones?" Mr. Barnett asks.

"Sentient?" Veronica asks. "Like they're alive?"

"Not technically," Mr. Barnett says. "But they are able to make choices. For instance, let's say a person was eating dinner alone in their co-op and suddenly they were choking on a piece of broccoli. The person is alone because they haven't been able to meet someone due to the taxing responsibilities of their job in accommodating all their boss's needs, because said boss promised me—I mean them—advancement after years of dedicated service. Polly would see that they were choking and would know to immediately call emergency services without being prompted."

"What's a co-op?" Jimmy asks.

"Would anyone else like to ask Polly a question?" Mr. Barnett says, avoiding Jimmy's gaze.

"Polly," Carolina asks. The metallic bird looks her way. "How many pollutants does Mammonton Industries emit in a calendar year?"

"Polly, shut off, please," Mr. Barnett says. Before the

bird can answer, its head turns down and the whirring noise stops. Mr. Barnett's phone vibrates. I look over and see the caller ID. It reads: OVERLORD WHO PAYS ME.

"Excuse me a moment," Mr. Barnett says, snatching his phone up and answering it. "Yes, sir." His smile starts to fade as he listens to the voice on the other end. "No, sir. I understand, sir. Yes, we are about to finish up. Oh! No, I can keep everyone here a while longer. Yes, sir. Keep me posted." Mr. Barnett hangs up the phone and puts it back in his pocket. "How would you all like to stay for lunch? I can order us takeout!"

"That's very generous of you," Mr. Hernandez says, still staring at Polly, "but we should be getting the kids back to school."

"Are you certain?" Mr. Barnett asks, turning his attention to Principal Li. "It's not every day we have guests and we have so enjoyed having you here." Has he? It feels like he was rushing to get us out earlier. "I know how much kids like pizza, right? Or maybe sushi? Or how about both! Sushi pizza!"

"I've had sushi pizza before," Veronica brags. I do like pizza and sushi, but I don't know how you combine the two. I'd like to try it, but not here and not with Polly watching us. I don't think I'd be able to swallow a bite.

"Bully for you, young lady!" Mr. Barnett says to Veronica, but his attention is still solely on Principal Li.

"Well, I don't know," she says uncertainly. "Some of the students do have tests this afternoon."

"Couldn't they be postponed?" Mr. Barnett asks.

"Yeah, they can!" Jimmy exclaims, and a bunch of kids laugh.

I hear Mr. Barnett's phone vibrate, and he retrieves it out of his pocket. He reads a text and from where I'm standing, I can read it too. It says *The asset has been acquired.*

"On second thought," Mr. Barnett says as he puts his phone away. "I wouldn't want to disrupt the little darlings' education. I will see you out!"

❋ ❋ ❋

Mr. Barnett walks us all the way back to the barrier before the security checkpoint. It's the fastest he's walked all day; we have to jog to keep up with him.

"Again, it was quite the experience having you here,"

Mr. Barnett says, standing by the doorway. He pushes a button on the wall to let us out. The doors slide open and we walk toward the guards. Our stuff is waiting for us in individual plastic crates stacked next to one another on the conveyor belt.

"Please thank Mr. Mammonton for us," Principal Li says. Mr. Barnett gently nudges her out. "I look forward to hearing from him regarding the endowment. Shall I call him tomorrow to make arrangements?"

"He'll be sure to get in touch when he has a moment," Mr. Barnett says as the last kid passes the threshold. "Okay, bye, kids! It's been real!" The solid doors slide shut. Carolina takes her backpack from a crate on the conveyor belt. She unzips it and looks inside. Then she approaches Herbie.

"Did you search our bags?" Carolina asks. "My folders aren't in the order they were in when I packed them."

"They probably just got shaken up a little," Herbie says with a small smirk. Carolina stares daggers at him and zips up her bag.

"Thanks for coming, folks," Herbie continues. "From

all of us at Mammonton Industries, we hope you have a great day."

We leave the security area and the guard who was behind the front desk stands to greet us. We start to leave the building, but I remember I need to dig out my key. I dash to the bathroom.

"Miss," the guard says. "Where are you off to?"

"I need to use the restroom," I say. The guard doesn't seem sympathetic. "I *really* got to go."

"Two minutes," the guard says. I rush inside the restroom.

When I get there, the only thing left of the potted plant is some dirt on the floor. It's gone! I look for it, panicking, hoping maybe somebody moved it under the sink or brought it into a stall as a prank. But why would anyone do that? There's a knock on the door.

"Time's up," the guard says.

"Lila, dear," Principal Li says. She's never called me *dear* before. "We really ought to be going."

I don't know what to do. I feel like crying.

"Everything okay, Lila?" I hear Ms. Zeller say. I want to tell her no, everything is not okay, but then I would have to explain about the key. Who would believe me? I leave the bathroom. Felise and Ms. Zeller are waiting for me while Principal Li thanks the guard. As soon as we get on the bus, it starts to rain.

"That is not a part of my forecast," Felise says as she sits down next to me. "I must be losing steam."

Chapter Thirteen

Our bus breaks down just before we reach the school parking lot. The driver doesn't know what's wrong, so we have to run for a bit in the rain to get back to school. Our clothes are soaked from the torrential downpour.

"Everybody here?" Mr. Hernandez asks. He counts all of us to make sure nobody got left behind in the rain as we enter the schoolhouse.

"Looks that way," Ms. Zeller says, also counting us one by one. "Okay, those of you who have gym clothes, you're going to want to change into them. Then we'll—" She stops once she notices dozens of frogs hopping all along the hallway and into classrooms. Kids who should be in class at this hour are shrieking with either delight or disgust.

"What is the meaning of this?" Principal Li asks to no one in particular. A frog lands on her shoe, and she lets out a yelp. Felise crouches down and picks the amphibian off Principal Li's foot.

"This is curious," Felise says to the frog, patting her finger over its slimy skin. Mr. Baxter, the science teacher, holds a jar with a few frogs inside it. He trails after another frog that's hopping down the hall.

"Mr. Baxter!" Principal Li shouts. Mr. Baxter looks up, stumbles, and the frogs in the jar fly out and into the air, one of them hitting Veronica right in the face. Veronica screams her head off, but the frog bounces off her forehead and lands relatively unharmed on the floor. Then it hops away.

"Principal Li, thank goodness you're back," Mr. Baxter says. "I don't know how this happened. I was sure the frogs were anesthetized. My eighth graders were meant to dissect them in class today, but they got loose somehow. The frogs, not the eighth graders. Though they also dispersed after the frogs got free."

"A lucky day for you, frog prince," Felise says to the little friend in her hand. "Only I did not foresee this happening." I swallow so hard I wonder if one of the runaway frogs ended up finding its way down my throat.

"Call Mr. McKenzie to help you . . . round them up," Principal Li says.

"I would," Mr. Baxter says, "but unfortunately he's busy with the fallout from the fire in the kitchen."

"Fire?!" Mr. Hernandez asks. "Should we evacuate the school?"

"Oh, no, my apologies! The fire is out now. No one was hurt. I didn't mean to worry you." Mr. Baxter's bow tie is askew and one of the elbow patches on his blazer is hanging by a thread. It looks like he's been through the wringer today. "But, well, I'm afraid the tater tots didn't make it."

"Not the tots!" Jimmy exclaims in abject horror. "What is this world coming to?"

"I must look into this," Principal Li says. "Ms. Zeller, will you see that the students change into suitable clothing before sending them off to class? Mr. Hernandez, if

you would help Mr. Baxter with collecting the speci-
mens." Then Principal Li rushes off to check on the
damage in the cafeteria kitchen.

I notice Felise doesn't hand Mr. Baxter her frog back.
Instead, she opens the door and lets it hop away into
the rain.

"All right, everybody," Ms. Zeller says. "Hurry up and
change into your dry clothes. You have ten minutes
before you're expected back in class. We have a math test
that counts for a third of your grade to get to."

"What?" I ask. I don't remember there being a test
today! "What test?"

"It's on the syllabus," Ms. Zeller says.

No, it wasn't! At least, I don't remember seeing a test
on there. A booming sound of thunder from outside rat-
tles my nerves even more.

"If the storm keeps going like this, I guess our game
will be canceled," Melanie says, sounding disappointed.
"My parents were going to come today."

"I'm sorry, Melanie," I say. Her parents can't always
make it to every game because of their jobs, and I know
how much it means to her when they cheer her on.

"It's not your fault," Melanie says. "You can't control the weather."

I can't, no, but my buddy Felise can—and right now she looks confused that things haven't gone the way she's planned.

"I'm going to go change into my sweats," Melanie says. "Are you coming?"

I take a few steps to join her, until Felise puts her hand on my shoulder.

"I believe Lila and I need a moment," she says. "We have something to discuss. In private." Melanie looks hurt, like we're excluding her. She doesn't know this is one conversation even I don't want to stick around for.

"Yeah. Okay. Whatever," Melanie says. "So much for having more than one good friend." She walks with the rest of the drenched students to their lockers.

"Melanie, wait!" I call out. But before I can try to explain myself to my oldest friend and squash whatever bad feelings might be bubbling up inside her, Felise pulls me into an empty classroom and shuts the door behind us.

"I cannot fathom what's happening," Felise says as she

paces back and forth in front of me. "Something is amiss. It's only the sixth day. Am I losing my touch? Mind you, it isn't as though this week was all that rigorous, considering your age and the scope of your ambitions. I mean, it isn't as though you were preparing for the Olympics or helming a rocket ship to outer space. Perhaps I'm out of practice?"

"Felise, relax," I say, trying to calm her down. "It's not your fault."

"I have honed my craft over countless years," Felise says, still pacing and ignoring me. "There's never been an incident like this before. Well, aside from that one time when the key was lost in 1929. It was most unfortunate to have the stock market crash, but that was years ago and—" She finally stops with her back to me. Then, slowly, Felise turns around. "Lila? You wouldn't by any chance have misplaced the key?"

"I wouldn't say misplaced," I say weakly. "I hid it."

"Do you mean to tell me the key is not currently in your possession?" Felise asks. Her voice is getting higher and her usually serene attitude is morphing into a panicked one.

"I buried it," I admit. "In a potted plant."

"We must retrieve it as soon as possible!" Felise says, inching closer to me. "Where is the plant?"

"At Mammonton Industries," I mumble. Felise's eyes get as large as tennis balls and her face is flushed.

"You left the key at that horrid place?" Felise asks. "Why would you do something so careless? This isn't like you, Lila. You're more responsible than that!" Felise starts to pace again, running her fingers through her hair. "I suppose I should have expected this. Children have not been bestowed with the gift of my abilities before. Perhaps it is because you are not quite ready to wield such power."

"Hey, hang on a minute," I say, offended on behalf of kids everywhere. "I thought you were *so* excited to be my age. If you did visit kids more often and sent some luck our way, this world would probably be a much kinder place!"

"You may be right," Felise says, whipping around to face me. "However, if we don't get that key back, we may not be able to find that out for quite some time. Seven years to be exact."

"So, I'll have bad luck for seven years?" I'm already not looking forward to being a teenager. I'm going to need all the luck I can get in high school.

"Not just you," Felise says. "It will impact every person around you, including this entire city and anyone who enters it. If I don't go through the door on the seventh day with the key, I will be stuck in this form for the duration of those seven years."

"You mean, you'll get to stay?" I ask, a little selfishly.

"As an eleven-year-old!" Felise shouts. "Please don't misunderstand me. I've had a marvelous time with you, but luck is *changeable*. It's fluid. I'm not meant to stay in one form for too long. I would not be my usual self either. My ability to provide good fortune would be gone! My joie de vivre would diminish! I would be a shell of myself, a husk with no purpose or home."

"You'd have a home with me," I say. Her eyes go back to their regular size. To my surprise, Felise's expression is warm.

"Really? Even if I weren't able to bring you any good tidings? Even if I was responsible for every calamity that may transpire in the next seven years?"

"I don't know. I'd miss hearing someone use words like *transpire* and *calamity* in everyday conversation if you weren't around." I grin. "It's been fun having you here. Even when you're not floating stuff around or making money appear left and right."

"That's very kind of you," Felise murmurs. "Albeit a bit naive. Nobody has ever . . . enjoyed my company without expecting something magical from me." She seems touched, but it doesn't last long. She shakes her head and tries to explain again. "Did you misplace the key on purpose? So that I would stay?"

"No!" I say. "I wouldn't do something that might hurt other people." I take a seat in an empty chair with a sigh. "In fact . . . *I* wasn't supposed to find you at all." She looks at me, not understanding, but she doesn't push me. Instead, Felise waits for me to say what I should have told her days ago. "I found the key in the Providential Hills Bank. Someone dropped it. I picked it up, thinking I would return it the next day. I didn't know any of this was supposed to happen. I didn't know you were going to show up and change my life. I wasn't supposed to have the key at all. It belongs to somebody else. I'm so sorry."

Felise steps closer to me. I think she's going to lecture me or tell me that I've ruined everything. Instead, she puts her hand on my arm.

"The key found *you*. Only you," she whispers. "And I am so lucky that it did."

"Really?" I wasn't expecting that. Maybe she's just saying that to make me feel better, but I don't think so. Not from the way she's looking at me.

"Really," she says with a nod. "Now, Lila joon, let's get that key back to its rightful owner."

Chapter Fourteen

We get on the 2:15 p.m. city bus to Mammonton Industries because the two o'clock bus left just as we were running to catch it.

"How come we can't, um, you know . . . ?" I say as I twirl my finger in the air and make a whoosh noise. "Get there faster."

"Teleportation is not in my repertoire," Felise says, apparently not caring if anyone else on the bus can hear us. "If you're wondering why a limousine didn't stop to pick us up and give us a free ride, my abilities diminish the farther away I am from the key. It's why I am almost always by your side."

"I thought it was because of my sparkling personality?" I joke. Felise is not amused. "Sorry. Just trying to brighten your mood."

"While I appreciate that, my mood will be improved once we find the key. Even my hair has begun to lose its luster." Felise holds up a lock for me to see. She's right. It isn't as bouncy as it usually is, and I think she has those things called split ends that Parisa is always trying to avoid.

The bus stops and we get off. We have to walk on foot for about five minutes to get to Mammonton Industries.

"Lucky I always have an umbrella in my locker, huh?" I say, opening it up for both of us to share. "See, I don't rely on you for everything." As soon as the words leave my mouth, I step into a giant puddle. My sock, shoe, and pant leg are soaked.

When we arrive at Mammonton Industries, there are fire trucks and ambulances parked outside the building.

"Oh dear," Felise says. We walk closer to the emergency service vehicles and see employees of Mammonton Industries running outside to join their co-workers who already evacuated.

"What's going on?" I ask a frazzled employee who has a giant coffee-colored stain splattered all over their shirt.

"All the technology has gone berserk," the employee says, staring at the building in fear.

"Is anybody hurt?" I ask.

"Not that I know of," the employee says, and for that I'm grateful. "But it's chaos in there! The Pollys have taken over!" The employee looks down in my direction. "What are you doing here, kid? Shouldn't you be at school?"

I should be doing a lot of things, like taking a mystery test that for sure wasn't on the syllabus and getting ready to help set up for tomorrow's bake sale. But because I didn't tell Felise about Mr. Mammonton earlier, I have a sneaking suspicion that this disaster is my fault.

I look to her for guidance on what we should do next, but she's already walking toward the entrance of the building. Felise doesn't pay attention to any of the temporary blockades or caution tape meant to keep people away.

"You can't go in there!" Herbie the security guard yells as I catch up to her. I expect him to turn us away from the plywood barricades.

"Of course I can." Felise snaps her fingers in front of his face, and to my surprise, Herbie lifts the caution tape.

"Go right ahead," he says in a dreamlike trance. We walk quickly past employees scrambling to get out. Felise dodges them effortlessly while I stay close behind her.

"Your powers must be coming back!" I say. "That was a cool Jedi mind trick you just pulled on that guard." We enter the now abandoned security area. There's no one manning the detectors.

"The closer I am to the key, the more I feel like my usual glorious self," she says. "Which reminds me, I was so proud of George when he put my mind trick in his screenplay. He worked so hard on it. I wonder how the film turned out?"

Before I can process that Felise may have helped birth one of the greatest media franchises in history, we arrive at the same open office space we'd visited only a few hours ago. Now it's in shambles. The laptops have burst into flames and a photocopy machine keeps spitting out reams of blank paper. The overhead lights flicker on and off. Employees make their way to the exits, some running away from flocks of attacking Polly drones.

"The square root of seven hundred fifty-three thousand is eight hundred sixty-seven point seven five five seven," one Polly bird declares in a feminine voice as it follows an employee wearing high heels and a pencil skirt.

"Make it stop!" the employee cries. One of her heels gets caught in the carpet. The shoe is left behind and the Polly bird swoops down to pick it up.

"Would you like your shoe back?" it asks. "I am Polly, here to assist you." The Polly bird clutches the shoe in its robotic talons, still pursuing the employee in the skirt.

Another employee wearing a vest and khakis is scurrying across the floor, but not fast enough. Another Polly swoops down and pours hot coffee on his back. The employee screams in pain as the coffee stains his shirt.

"Black, two sugars. Just the way you like it," the Polly who dropped the coffee cup says in a masculine voice. Then it lets out an unbearable squawk that makes me cover my ears with my hands. There are hundreds of the mechanical birds zipping around at dangerous speeds, chasing employees and either attacking them with beverages or spitting out annoying facts nobody asked for.

"That's the problem with humans and innovation," Felise says, not at all affected by the chaos. "Your kind always ask yourselves if you *can* build something, but never whether you should."

A Polly heads our way with a soda can in its clutches, ready to pour carbonated liquid sugar all over us.

"No libations for my friend and me, thank you," Felise says. She waves her hand in the air. The Polly crashes into a wall, falls to the ground, and cracks into pieces. "The key is close. I can sense it. Feel free to loosen your grip at any time." I realize I'm squeezing her arm pretty tightly.

"Sorry," I say. I let go but stay right behind her, on high alert for any more Pollys that might be headed our way. We continue to walk the route of our tour from earlier in the day. When we reach the giant window that overlooks the factory floor, we find Mr. Barnett sipping from a Styrofoam cup. (Which I didn't think they made anymore because they're super bad for the environment.) He stares down at the conveyor belts.

"Mr. Barnett?" I ask. "Is everything okay?"

He continues to gaze through the window, his forced smile nowhere to be seen. He looks a lot paler than he did this morning.

"I had dreams once," Mr. Barnett says, more to himself than to us. "Then I started working here. I figured I'd devote my youth to my work, dedicate myself to my duties, and ascend the corporate ladder. I'd get to oversee a few acquisitions, maybe. Then I'd no longer have to cater to the wishes of an overbearing boss. I even thought I'd cash in on the vacation days I never use. I've heard Hawaii is beautiful."

"It really is," Felise whispers to me. "I had a wonderful time in Oahu."

"Now I see that everything is so fragile," Mr. Barnett continues, still looking down at the factory floor. Felise and I take a step closer to see what he's so focused on. The conveyor belts are moving at lightning speed, smoke billowing up as the belts carry unassembled parts with nowhere to go and send them crashing to the floor. Whatever product the factory was putting together is piling up in pieces. The machines and robots are malfunctioning—some of them on fire, some continuing to go through their programmed motions but smashing the conveyor belts instead of moving things along.

We look back at Mr. Barnett. He takes another sip from his cup, but his hand trembles when he lifts it to his lips.

"This will set the company back, oh . . . I don't know. Months? Years? It doesn't matter, though. I'll probably be fired once the literal and figurative smoke clears."

"Sir," I say softly. I haven't had the greatest impression of Mr. Barnett, but I can't help but feel a little sorry for the guy. "Could you tell us where we can find Mr. Mammonton? It's kind of important." I don't expect him to help us, considering he looks pretty zoned in on the catastrophe below. But he does.

"Take the private elevator on the left to the top floor," he says, still not looking at us. We walk slowly past him, not wanting to upset him further.

"It's never too late to forge a new career path," Felise says to him. "I have a feeling you'll find another job when you're ready."

Mr. Barnett turns his head and gives us a genuine, if weak, smile.

"You think?"

"I know," Felise says. She makes a two-fingered salute.

"I hope you get to see Hawaii!" I call out over my shoulder as I follow her to the elevator.

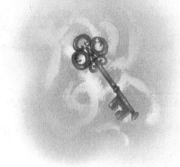

Chapter Fifteen

When the private elevator door opens, we enter a huge study. It's just as cold and full of steel and granite as the rest of the building, only here there's a single piece of art. A framed oil painting of Mr. Mammonton sitting in an armchair hangs on a wall, looming over the real Mr. Mammonton, who is sitting in the exact same armchair. It's like having double vision, except the oil painting isn't holding a bronze key the way the real Mr. Mammonton is.

Felise doesn't wait for an invitation from the scowling mogul to enter his office. She takes long, confident strides toward his desk. The potted plant from the bathroom rests beside it. That's what Mr. Barnett's *The asset has been acquired* text meant! The cameras in the lobby must have seen me go into the restroom before the tour started.

"I believe you have something that belongs to my friend," Felise says, her voice still lilting and cheerful as she nods at the key in his hand.

Mr. Mammonton holds my necklace with his index finger, dangling the key in front of us. A tiny grin shows a few of his gray and sharp teeth. He's dressed in his usual black suit and tie, but whatever is left of his hair is sticking up in all directions. A trickle of sweat drips down his temple.

"Do you mean this?" Mr. Mammonton asks. "I think not. This is my property. I paid for it to be found. It belongs to me."

Felise takes a step closer, not at all intimidated by the powerful man in front of her.

"I am asking you politely," she says, her voice strong. "But even my manners have limits. I can assure you it is not in your best interest to test those limits."

Mr. Mammonton lets out a noise from his mouth that

I think is meant to be a laugh, but it's so dry and garbled it sounds like he might be coughing. He doesn't strike me as someone who has lots of experience in the humor department.

"Why would I take orders from a child? Do you know who I am? What kind of empire I have built? What I have done to those who have dared to get in my way?" Mr. Mammonton puffs out his chest.

"I cannot say I have ever given you much thought," Felise says, looking at her fingernails. She's clearly not paying Mr. Mammonton the respect he feels he deserves. "I am, however, running out of patience. And I'm going to need the key back."

Mr. Mammonton's face turns pink and his teeth clench, but then he leans back in his chair, assessing Felise.

"You're the being, aren't you?" he asks her, but it looks like he already knows the answer. "The avatar that the key summons?"

"My reputation precedes me," Felise says before she lets out a long yawn.

"I expected more," Mr. Mammonton says. "I've gone

to great lengths to harness your powers. I spent thirty years on the hunt, hiring crews on seven continents, searching for you with all the resources at my disposal. What a disappointment to find that you are nothing more than a little girl."

Mr. Mammonton lets out more grunts and hacks that I'm pretty sure are his version of laughter. When the noises subside, Felise straightens her shoulders and gives him her full attention.

"Evidently you have no idea what power *little girls* have inside them," Felise says. Mr. Mammonton wipes at the corner of his eye. He coughs out a few more chuckles before he speaks again.

"The key is mine," Mr. Mammonton says, banging his fist down on his desk. "*You* are mine. So, if you would be so kind as to dismiss the child who stole you from me, we can begin the work of conquering my enemies and growing my empire to its highest heights."

Felise interlocks her fingers in front of her and stretches her arms. The crack that comes from her knuckles echoes throughout the room.

"I don't belong to anyone," Felise says, lowering her

hands and balling them into fists. "It is true that I've aided some who were not deserving of my abilities, but the key found Lila this time. I am at *her* service until tomorrow. As you can see, since you've taken the key from her, your building is in disarray. But this is only a fraction of the ruin you will face if you don't back down. You must return the key to her. Otherwise, I'll be forced to unleash a wrath of misfortune upon you that will last for the entirety of your miserable life."

"Do you think me a fool?" Mr. Mammonton asks, now leaning forward in his chair. He puts his hand over the key and slams it down on his desk. "This is what I am entitled to! This is what I have been searching for! I am a captain of industry, with a reach that you do not seem to grasp. I am a man feared by titans! Why would you waste your superior gifts on a child who knows nothing of what this world has to offer?"

"Um, excuse me," I say, stepping forward and standing beside Felise. "Hi, sorry to interrupt your villainous monologue, but, um, well, it seems like you've had plenty of good fortune so far. Given, you know, all the money and power and all. Don't you feel like you have enough?"

Mammonton looks at me like I'm the biggest loser in the whole world. I'm not quite sure how I've summoned the courage to speak like this to a man who is both scary and could probably buy his own private island, but having Felise here helps.

"Anyway," I continue, "I really need the key back for my friend here. She's helped me and my community out a lot this week. Whoever she finds next, I hope they know how to help others with their good fortune, the way she's helped me." Felise takes my hand in hers and I squeeze it. "Also, your parrot robot things are tearing the place apart downstairs. Don't know if you have a plan for that or . . ." Mr. Mammonton sneers at me. I squeeze Felice's hand again. "Never mind."

"Lila joon," Felise says, turning to me and giving me a gentle smile. "It seems Mr. Mammonton is in need of a tad more clarity." She lets go of my hand. "Would you mind giving me a little space so I can show him who he is dealing with?"

"Oh! Sure thing," I say. I take a step to the side.

"A smidge more," Lila says. I take another step. "Sorry. Just one more big step." I do what she asks. "Wonderful. Would you mind bracing yourself? And hold on to something that is securely fastened to the floor." I wrap my arms around a column with a statue of Mr. Mammonton's head on it. I think it's called a bust, which I never understood. Anyway, I hold on tight, even though I don't know exactly what Felise has in store for him.

"This okay?"

"That's perfect—just like you," Felise says, her voice honeysuckle sweet. "Thank you. Please hold on. This will only take a moment." Felise clears her throat, then tilts her head from side to side. Her neck cracks, and she rolls her shoulders like a boxer getting ready for a fight. "If you won't take me seriously in this form—which you should, but alas I cannot remedy your sexism or ageism—perhaps you will heed a form you're more accustomed to."

Felise stretches and twists and turns. I can hear her bones crunch and contort as her body grows larger in width and height. Her skin becomes a lighter shade;

some of her hair falls out and the rest turns gray. The gold dress and sneakers with wings on them transform into a black suit and tie. She has turned into the mirror image of Mr. Mammonton.

"Uncanny," Mr. Mammonton cries out, his mouth open in shock. I should be afraid of Felise now that she looks like him, but she gives me a wink to let me know she's still in there. Then she faces off with the real Mammonton again.

"Now, I am going to give you an example of what bad fortune will befall you if you do not release the key." Felise's voice is now deep and hoarse, just like Mr. Mammonton's. A newspaper appears out of thin air and lands on his desk. "Read aloud the date on the front page."

Mr. Mammonton doesn't move a muscle.

"I would not try my patience if I were you," Felise says. "And unfortunately, I *am* you for the time being."

Oooooh, good one, Felise! Mr. Mammonton picks up the paper with the hand that isn't holding on to the key.

"This is dated a year from now," he mutters.

"What does the headline say?" Mammonton's double asks.

"Mammonton Industries files for bankruptcy," Mr. Mammonton reads in a loud voice. It doesn't sound like he's taking it all that seriously. He tosses the paper down. "This is simply a parlor trick."

"You know what I am," Felise says. "You have deciphered in the ancient texts what I am capable of. I do not *trick*."

The real Mr. Mammonton sits up in his chair a little, another trickle of sweat forming, this time on his forehead. A magazine replaces the newspaper on the desk.

"Read it."

Mr. Mammonton peers at the cover first before picking it up with both hands. He pulls it close to his face, which is quickly turning cherry red.

"Those jackals!" Mr. Mammonton exclaims. "They can't buy my company just to tear it apart, piece by piece!"

"I'm afraid your competitors can acquire your entire empire, should your luck be on a downward swing," Felise says, placing a hand on her hip.

"You think this intimidates me?" Mammonton asks. He throws the magazine in Felise's direction. It doesn't make it—simply disappearing as though it were never there. "I've gone toe to toe with heads of state," he continues in a rant. "I've buried tycoons who got too big for their britches. I've seen businesses come and go and *I* have lasted. You can't scare me."

Felise lets out a weary sigh.

"Well, I sure can try," Felise says. The room suddenly grows dark. I look up and see clouds forming above us— *inside* the building. A bolt of lightning flashes. It strikes the portrait of Mr. Mammonton hanging on the wall behind him. Mr. Mammonton jumps out of his seat and turns to watch the painting burn to a crisp. The room fills with the deafening sound of thunder. I want to cover my ears, but I remember that Felise told me to hold on tight. That's what I plan on doing until this demonstration of hers is over. The clouds break open and freezing rain starts to pour down fast and hard. The rain doesn't do much to put out the burning painting, but the water is rising. The room will flood in no time. I shiver, water coming up to my knees.

"I will not give in!" Mr. Mammonton shouts. Droplets of rain drip down the sides of his head. His suit is completely soaked. "Do you hear me? I. WILL. NOT. GIVE. IN!"

A strong wind begins to blow and Mr. Mammonton loses his balance, landing on his back. I hug the column tight as it starts to shake.

"HEAR ME NOW, GREEDY PEON," Felise howls in a voice so low and loud it isn't human. She sounds like a monster from a horror movie, one that's R-rated and full of gory violence, the kind that I'm not allowed to see. Mr. Mammonton lifts his head, but he's on his knees, staring up at Felise. She begins to levitate off the ground, floating in the air with her arms extended on either side of her. Her version of Mr. Mammonton's eyes turns fiery red, and her version of Mr. Mammonton's teeth grows longer and sharper. "RETURN THE KEY TO THE RIGHTFUL OWNER OR SUFFER THE CONSEQUENCES OF MY WRATH!"

The real Mr. Mammonton gawks at the monstrous version of himself. His lower lip trembles. Felise as vampire-Mammonton lets out a high-decibel screech.

Her skin begins to disintegrate and turns to dust! She sheds Mr. Mammonton's body and morphs into a glowing skeleton, writhing in the air in pain. I close my eyes because it's too horrible to look at.

"Stop!" Mr. Mammonton calls out. "No more! I believe!"

The rain and wind slowly abate, but I still hang on to the column for dear life. I feel a hand on my shoulder and flinch.

"It's all right," Felise says. She's back to the way she was when I first met her. The room looks like it did before she created a storm. My clothes are dry and the painting isn't burned to ash. But it *is* different. In the portrait, Mr. Mammonton doesn't look as confident and serious as he did when we entered. He looks distressed and unsure. I glance back at Felise. Her eyes are warm and apologetic. "I'm sorry if I frightened you."

"Me? Frightened?" I squeak out. "I knew it was all going to be okay." She smiles at me and rubs my shoulder.

"You can let go whenever you're ready," Felise says softly.

"Oh. Right," I say, unclenching more than just my arms. Felise takes me by the hand and walks us toward the exit.

Once we reach it, she slowly turns around. "Now, Mr. Mammonton . . . the key."

Mr. Mammonton is still on his knees, shaking partly because he's freaked out and partly because his clothes are still wet.

"Y-y-yessss," he says, holding his hands up. The necklace with the key drops to the floor.

"Hold out your hand," Felise whispers to me. I do as she says. The key floats up and toward us, finally hovering in the air right above my palm. I put the necklace around my neck, relieved to have it back.

"Congratulations, Mr. Mammonton," Felise says. "Your luck has not yet run out. By the way, I do hope you won't be rescinding your offer to help fund programs at Lila's school?"

Mr. Mammonton shakes his head, his glasses slipping off his nose and falling to the floor.

"Excellent. In the future, I do hope you will find ways to help the environment, and civilization as a whole, with your products." Felise links her arm with mine. "Oh, and regarding your assistant, Mr. Barnett. He seems incredibly overworked. I imagine he is due for a paid vacation, no?"

With that, we leave Mr. Mammonton in his office with a lot to think about.

Chapter Sixteen

"How much did we make?" Jimmy asks Mr. Hernandez as he totals all the money from the bake sale.

"Shhh, let Mr. Hernandez count," Veronica says. Then she breaks off another chunk of leftover bran muffin and stuffs it in her mouth. I knew bran muffins weren't going to sell.

It was smart to have the bake sale outside the school entrance. We sold almost everything to lots of happy customers passing by on the sidewalk. And the baklava my family and I made went like hot cakes! Well, not hot cakes. Nobody made any of those. But the baklava was a hit.

"We did really well," Mr. Hernandez says, finishing

up his tally. "Our grand total is five hundred sixty-five dollars and thirty-five cents!"

"Nice!" Jimmy says. "We did it!"

"No, we didn't," Carolina says, doing the math in her head. "With the money Lila donated and the money from ticket sales for our concert, we're still short by about two thousand dollars."

"Bummer," Jimmy says, deflating in his seat like a bicycle tire punctured by a nail.

"What about the money Mr. Mammonton said he was going to give us?" Veronica asks.

"We don't know if he'll actually do it," Carolina says. "Or when."

"Trust me, he will," Felise says in between bites of her shrimp empanada.

"With what happened to his factory yesterday, our music program may not be his top priority right now," says Mr. Hernandez. "But we should be proud of ourselves! We came so close and we didn't give up! Not to mention we have the concert to look forward to." He's doing his best to be optimistic, but I can tell he's disappointed too.

"We could find another way to raise money," I suggest. Felise looks at me with pride. "Like a car wash!"

"That's true," Carolina says. "We still have time before the semester is over."

"Yeah! It's not impossible," I say. "I mean, it'll take a lot of effort, but if we work together we can come up with something. The band doesn't have to break up yet."

"I hope not," Jimmy says. "My parents finally said I can play the drums if I want to. I'd sell my oboe to help out, but my mom wants to hang on to it, in case I have an overnight personality change and want to pick it up again."

"In three," I hear Felise say under her breath. She's staring hard at her empanada as she counts. "Two, one." Felise then points her index finger at someone walking toward us.

"Excuse me," the passerby says.

"Hello," Mr. Hernandez says. "We're just about finished with the bake sale."

"May I interest you in a bran muffin?" Veronica says, holding the mostly full tray up to the stranger. "They're very good."

"Oh, uh, no," the wanderer says. "I'm not here for that.

I'm all about the keto plan these days. I'm here to buy the lawn mower. I'm supposed to meet someone named Felise?"

"What?" Mr. Hernandez asks.

The keto enthusiast (whatever keto is) holds up his phone. There's an ad with a photo of the lawn mower I won from the ShopTilYouDrop contest.

"Frank? Hi, I'm Felise," my always-surprising friend says. "The lawn mower is parked right on the soccer field behind the schoolhouse. Would you like me to show it to you?"

"Oh, I can find it," Frank says, shaking hands with Felise. "Is a check okay?"

"It certainly is," Felise says. Frank hands a folded check from his pocket to her.

"Thanks a lot." Frank heads over to the soccer field and Felise hands the check to me.

"I hope you don't mind my placing the ad," she whispers. "You *did* mention you weren't sure what you were going to do with a lawn mower."

I unfold the check and see it's made out to the Providential Hills Middle School Arts Fund for $1,777. I look up and find everybody staring at me in anticipation.

"And the beat goes on," I say. Everyone cheers and jumps and dances.

"I will miss this," Felise says, picking a piece of lint off her shoulder and dropping it on the grass. But she lets out a happy shriek when I take her by the hand and bring her into our hopping huddle, all of us chanting her name in appreciation.

"We should celebrate!" Mr. Hernandez shouts as he jumps with us. "Pizza's on me!"

"Pizza!" Felise says. "Nectar from the heavens!"

The sun begins to set as Felise and I walk home together. I'm holding empty trays under my arms and a Ziploc bag full of baklava. Felise carries a box of pizza on her hip and a slice of pineapple, pepperoni, goat cheese, and onion pizza folded up in her hand to snack on.

"I was not present for the creation of pizza, so unfortunately I cannot take credit for that," she says. "But whoever came up with it is a genius." Felise takes a big bite of her slice. She talks with her mouth full, tomato sauce stuck to the corner of her lip.

"Five boxes in one sitting must be a new record," I say. I don't think Mr. Hernandez expected Felise to put away *so* much pizza when he offered to pay, but luckily most of it was comped by the restaurant's manager. Her son used to play trombone at Providential Hills Middle School.

"It is . . . unclear when I will get to enjoy pizza again," Felise says, taking another giant bite. "We must make the most of the opportunities we're given."

I feel an ache in my chest. She's going away soon. Forever. I can't even write her an email or call her up to see how she's doing or talk about what happened at school. I don't know where she'll end up. She doesn't really either.

"Lila? Are you going to ring the bell, or shall I?"

"Oh. Right." We're standing on Melanie's doorstep. I push the button. While we wait for someone to answer the door, Felise finishes the slice in her hand. Good thing she has about seven more in the box she's holding, in case she's still hungry before we get home.

Melanie opens the door when she sees us, but not all the way.

"Hi," I say.

"Hey," she says back, opening it a little wider but not inviting us in.

"I saved these for you," I say, holding up the Ziploc bag of baklava. "Didn't see you at the bake sale."

"Thanks." She takes the bag. "I didn't feel up to it."

I guess she's still upset about Felise and me leaving her out of our talk yesterday. I want to explain to her that I'd never exclude her from anything, except when it comes to making sure the luck of Providential Hills doesn't go down the drain for seven years.

But then she turns to Felise. "Hi, I'm Melanie."

I'm confused, but before I can ask Melanie why she's introducing herself, Felise waves.

"Hello, Melanie," she says. "I'm Felise. I was visiting Lila from out of town, but I must be going soon." Felise grins brightly. "I just *had* to meet you before I left, though. You mean a great deal to Lila."

"She means a lot to me too," Melanie says, laughing a little in discomfort.

"She talks about you all the time," Felise says.

"I—I'd like to say she's talked about you a lot too,"

Melanie says. Her eyes search for some memory of Felise, but I can guess by now that she won't find any. "Are you a friend from the summer or something?"

"Or something, yes," Felise says, her smile dimming. "Lila may be a little morose once I leave. You know how it can be when a friend goes away, particularly one as sensational as moi. I wonder if you wouldn't mind spending some quality time with her to ease her pain?"

"Sure, I'd love to," Melanie says. Then she turns to me. "Want to come over tomorrow? We can watch a movie or start a puzzle or something. We haven't done that in a while."

"Yeah, that'd be great," I say.

"You know"—Melanie begins. She's smiling at me, but her eyebrows bunch together—"I was kind of mad at you earlier, only I can't remember what for?"

"I'm sure it was simply a misunderstanding," Felise says. "Friends may argue sometimes, but true friendship can always see its way through any obstacle. No matter the distance." Felise looks my way when she says this last part. It takes everything in me not to start bawling.

"Okayyyyy," Melanie says. "Do you two want to come in for a minute?"

"That's very kind of you," Felise says. "But we should be going. I have an engagement that unfortunately cannot be put off. I'll give you two a moment alone." Felise extends her hand for Melanie to shake, which she does. "It was so good to meet you. I wish you a long and fortuitous soccer career."

"Thanks," Melanie says brightly. Felise walks away from us and waits for me on the sidewalk.

"Does your friend always talk like that?" Melanie asks.

"Does she ever," I say with a laugh. "But you get used to it."

"She seems pretty cool," Melanie says.

"Mel, do you remember anything about this week?" I ask. Melanie thinks about it for a moment.

"Yeah, um, we beat the Jaguars and celebrated with ice pops after. We went to the ShopTilYouDrop to get stuff for the bake sale and you won all those prizes. Oh, and you went viral on the internet shooting hoops! That was so wild! I still don't know how you did it. Why do you ask?"

She didn't mention Felise once.

"No reason," I say. "I just wanted to make sure I didn't dream up how awesome this week was."

"Hey, I'll always be around to pinch you awake," she says. "See you tomorrow?"

I don't know if I'll be great company, but it'll be good to spend time with my oldest friend once my newest one is gone forever.

"I'll bring popcorn," I say.

Felise is uncharacteristically quiet during our walk to my house, but that's okay. I don't feel much like talking either.

"Hi, Lila joon," Mom calls from the living room when we walk through the front door. "How was the bake sale?"

"The game is about to start," I hear Dad say.

Felise and I join them there. My parents are sitting on the couch, ready to watch our favorite basketball team on TV. Parisa sits on the comfy recliner chair, typing and swiping on her phone.

"Oh, hello," Mom says, rising from her spot on the

couch. "I'm Mrs. Moradi." Mom shakes Felise's hand. Parisa looks up.

"It is an absolute honor to know you," Felise says. She holds up the box of pizza. "We took the liberty of bringing you dinner."

"That's awfully thoughtful of you," Dad says, also standing up and taking the box from Felise. "Um, I'm sorry, would you remind me of your name?"

"She didn't tell us," Parisa says, looking up at Felise. "Who's your friend, Lila?"

It's like what Felise said when she first came into my life. Nobody will remember she'd been here.

"This is Felise," I say. "She's one of the best friends I'll ever have."

"Really?" Felise asks, turning her head to me.

"Really," I say. Both of us start to cry.

Mom rushes over and wraps her arms around both of our shoulders.

"Oh, girls, what's wrong?" she asks, rubbing my back.

Dad sets the pizza down and leaves the room. He comes back with a box of tissues. Parisa stays in her seat, but she puts her phone away.

"Nothing," Felise says, tears still streaming down her eyes. "We are processing overwhelming human emotions like gratitude, melancholy, and love. This is all quite new. It hasn't really happened to me before."

"Is it because this is your first time being eleven?" I ask.

Dad gives me a confused glance. He takes the trays from the bake sale and passes me the tissue box. I take two, one for me and one for Felise. She accepts hers and blows her nose so loudly I bet people in the next neighborhood can hear it.

"No," she says. "It's not hormone related." Dad looks a little uncomfortable. "You've all been so wonderful." She gazes up at my mom, who is still holding on to us. "Your daughter really got to me. In here," Felise says, pointing at her heart. "You've raised her well."

"Um—thank you," Mom says.

"She's our sunshine," Dad chimes in, smiling at both of us. This gets Felise worked up again, crying into the tissue that should be snotty but isn't. "Oh no! What did I say?"

"She *is* sunshine!" Felise wails. "Even when she's

doubting herself or uptight, she still wants the best for everyone around her."

"Not everyone," I say. "Mr. Mammonton was kind of a jerk."

"Who?" Dad asks, his eyes wide. Felise laughs through her tears and I wipe mine away. She catches her breath, composes herself, and straightens her posture.

"I wish you all nothing but health, happiness, and many years filled with laughter and love for one another," Felise says. "Even you, Parisa, you competitive-beyond-reason dynamo, you."

"Hey!" Parisa says. "Wait a minute—how do you know my name?"

"I got to know you through Lila," Felise explains. "The way she's described all of you, of course. Not from ever having lovely dinners or sharing in fun domestic activities in your household. I feel like I've always known you all."

Mom holds Felise closer.

"You know . . ." Mom says. "It's the oddest thing, but I feel the same way." Felise leans into my mother's embrace.

"Haven't we met you before?" Dad asks. "You seem very familiar."

"Yeah, you do," Parisa says, squinting at Felise. "Do you go to Lila's school?"

"A lovely place, but no," Felise says. "I typically reside in the ether of an astral plane that mortals will never be able to find." My family doesn't say anything—and who could blame them? "It does not matter how or where we met, though. What matters is that we have."

"I get it!" Parisa says, snapping her fingers. "You're a theater kid. Nice to see you broadening your social horizons, Lila."

"Why don't we all sit down and get better acquainted?" Dad offers. "Do you like basketball, Felise? If not, we can watch something else? Whatever you like."

"I'd love to join you," Felise says. "But we have to be heading upstairs. I only popped in to say good—to say hello."

"You're always welcome here," Mom says and gives Felise another squeeze. When she finally lets us go, Felise takes one last look at my family, then turns around and slowly walks up the stairs.

"She seems very sweet," Dad says to me.

"And offbeat," Parisa chimes in. "But her outfit is pretty dope."

"Are you sure she's okay?" Mom asks. I nod so they don't worry. I want them to think nothing's wrong. But really, I feel like everything is.

❊ ❊ ❊

Felise and I sit next to each other on the edge of my bed. My futon isn't on the floor. I don't know who put it away, but I guess I won't be needing it anymore.

"Do you, um . . ." I begin. "Do you know where you're going to next?"

"No," Felise says, staring at the carpet. "The box does land somewhere near the last person to have found it."

She looks up at me. I can't see the sparkle in her eyes anymore, the one that was there on the first day of her arrival.

"It's never been quite fair, I suppose. Once the box appears, those with knowledge of its nature and the resources to acquire it always have the upper hand. It's a cycle of unfair opportunity. Usually, I've been found by a lot of older men. But now, I think things might change. I hope, anyway. Thanks to you."

"Well, whoever finds you," I whisper, "they're lucky to have a friend like you. And not just because of all the, well, you know . . ." I twirl my index finger in the air and make a whooshing noise.

"Is that what I look like when I use magic?" Felise asks with a horrified laugh.

"No." I laugh too, to keep from crying again. "You're a bit more graceful."

"I should say so." Felise brushes make-believe dust off her shoulder. She looks at the Caruso the Chipmunk clock on my wall. "It's almost time." She slides off the bed and I do the same. "Will you read the poem inside the key's box and memorize it?"

I pull the box out from my nightstand drawer. Once, I'd thought it was ordinary. I read the inside, committing the words to memory as best I can.

"Okay," I say, repeating the words silently to myself. "I've got it."

"Excellent," she says. "Now would you please place it on the floor in the center of the room."

I walk the box to where she's told me to and gently

lower it to the floor. I walk backward slowly, not sure what's supposed to happen. I don't want to say or do the wrong thing and have Felise suffer some magical consequence.

Felise and I stand next to each other, both of us just looking at the box.

"Do you mind if I play some outro music?" she asks.

I shake my head. She waves her hand and a song plays in the room. I don't know where it's coming from since I don't have any speakers, but none of that matters now.

"It's called 'History Repeating,'" she says. "By the Propellerheads and Shirley Bassey."

I've never heard it before, but it's brassy and bold and wise. It's a Felise jam for sure.

"Now," she says, "would you take off your necklace and hold it up in your palm?"

I pull the chain over my head and place the key in my open hand, raising it up as an offering.

"When you are ready, recite the poem you have just learned."

I'm about to say it aloud when Felise stops me. "Wait! Are you a hugger?"

"What?!" I ask. I'm nervous as it is without being interrupted.

"I want to bid you farewell," Felise says. "But I know some people prefer to keep their personal space to themselves."

"Hugs are okay," I say. "Even if they are for saying goodbye."

"Just checking," Felise says. "You may continue."

I clear my throat and start to speak the words. "Now it is time to depart, but may you always have luck in your heart!"

The key shakes against my palm and comes alive. It floats into the air, hovering just above my lifeline. The box opens and a bright, otherworldly light bursts out of it. The colors of the light change and swirl until an almost blinding golden beam makes an open doorway appear. On the other side of the doorway is a constellation of stars. It looks like the Milky Way, if its stars were all the colors of the rainbow. The key quickly speeds away from my hand and to the door's keyhole, clicking itself inside and waiting for Felise to walk through. She turns to face me.

"I am so lucky to have met you, Lila Moradi," Felise says.

I beat her to the hug, leaping toward her and pulling her in tight—wishing she didn't have to leave me.

"You are a force of strength!" she says, stumbling backward a little. Then she squeezes me tightly too.

"I'll miss you so much," I say.

She's the first to let go. She takes my chin in her hand.

"I will miss you too," Felise says. "Though I can do without middle school homework. That I won't miss." She kisses my cheek. "And who knows? Maybe our paths will cross again."

Felise pinches my nose and honks. I'd tell her to cut it out, but not today. She then glides to the door, perfectly in time with the beat of the song.

To leave me and my life behind.

"Good luck, Felise!" I call out as she stands in the doorway. She looks over her shoulder and gives me one last stunner of a smile.

"Luck is what you make of it," she says. "Remember: Where you find opportunity, that's where you'll find me.

Always." Then she turns her head, steps inside the door, and closes it shut behind her.

The song stops playing. The key turns in the lock. Suddenly, the glowing door is sucked back into the box, which closes just as quickly as it opened. Before I can move a muscle, the box dissolves into dust, departing for places unknown.

I'm alone again in my ordinary room. It's too quiet . . . until I hear sounds of the TV from downstairs. I know if I stay in here, I'll start crying again. So I walk down and join my family in the living room.

"Lila? When did you get home?" Mom asks. "I was getting worried. I was about to call Mr. Hernandez."

"I . . . I saw you when I came in," I say. "With Felise."

"Who's Felise?" Parisa asks, her eyes on the TV. They don't remember.

"She—never mind," I say. I walk over to the couch and sit in between my parents.

They may not remember her, but I'll never forget.

Chapter Seventeen

"What do you think of this?" Cassandra asks me. She holds up her drawing of a character from the anime show we both like.

"Whoa, that's sick," Jimmy says, looking up from a comic book.

It's been a few months since Felise left. At first it was hard to be without her. Not just because I got pop quizzes again, or stepped in gum and she wasn't there to clean it up. But because it was hard finding friends who could fill the void she left.

That's why I started a new club at school. It's called Tooning Out, and so far it's been awesome!

"I really like your use of bold colors, Cassandra," Ms. Zeller, our club advisor, says.

She's sitting at a brand-new desk, part of the five hundred provided by Mammonton Industries. I was surprised she agreed to be Tooning Out's faculty mentor, but I was more surprised to discover that she's a huge fan of old cartoon shows. When she was our age, Ms. Zeller used to watch shows like *Daria* and *Batman: The Animated Series*. She brings old DVDs to the club sometimes and shows them to us.

We don't have a set number of members in our club, but that's cool because everyone is welcome. Nobody has to audition or know anything about comics or animation to join. Students can pop in whenever they like.

We have repeat members like Cassandra and Jimmy, but we also have people who just want to show up once in a while, like Melanie and Veronica. We draw, talk about any new manga or graphic novels we're reading, and some days just watch cartoons that have historical merit to the craft of animation. We even write up reports about the history of animation and present them in homeroom for credit.

It's been a blast to start the club and see it grow. Even if it isn't considered the coolest activity at school. (That honor belongs to French club because they're always eating crepes and baguettes.) *I* think it's the coolest, though, and it's been great to find like-minded kids.

"I was thinking," Cassandra says, passing her drawing to Jimmy, "maybe we could start our own comic strip. And if it's good enough, we can even ask to put it in the school newspaper."

"That's a great idea!" I say. I'm not supergood at drawing, but I am getting better. I bet I could write up stories and characters for the strip, though.

"Can it be about a kid who's a rock star drummer but secretly also a space alien on the run from intergalactic bandits?" Jimmy asks.

"It could be . . ." Cassandra says. "But I was thinking it'd be about stuff going on at school. Like the Clovers sports teams." Soccer season is over, but Cassandra is already in lacrosse mode.

"A comic strip about jocks?!" Jimmy asks. "Can the jocks at least be radioactive?"

The bell rings and the three of us let out a groan. It's always sad when Tooning Out is over, even on a Friday, the best school day of the week.

"That's something to think about over the weekend," Ms. Zeller says, pulling out a book from her purse. "Before I forget—Lila, the book you asked me to request from the school library came in."

She passes me a thick nonfiction book called *The Queens of Animation: The Untold Story of the Women Who Transformed the World of Disney and Made Cinematic History* by Nathalia Holt.

"Hey, that's great, Ms. Zeller!" I say. "It's my lucky day."

"Or it just showed up once someone returned it," Ms. Zeller says. She's not much for the fantastical. "Have a good weekend, Lila."

Parisa leads me and my friends to our aisle in the concert arena. Melanie and Carolina follow and we get in our assigned seats for Pop Fest 3000.

I had a lot of trouble deciding who to take. I only had two tickets from winning the basketball shooting contest and I wanted to invite Melanie, but I knew Parisa would be bummed if she missed the coolest live music event around. Thankfully, my parents were really sweet. They made my life easier by buying two extra tickets. I have to take out the trash for a month, in addition to my other chores, but it's worth it so no one feels left out.

"Amazing!" Melanie says. "These seats are so close."

"I've had better seats," Parisa says—because of course she has. "We got here way too early. The opening act doesn't go on for another half an hour."

She's right. There aren't too many people here yet, but fans are slowly milling into the huge arena. It's my first concert and I can't wait to hear how loud it will get!

"Thanks for inviting me, Lila," Carolina says.

"I know how much music means to you," I say. "How's band, by the way?"

Our concert was a huge success. We didn't sound too bad anyway. But I also decided the triangle isn't really for me. I still like to hear my former bandmates play in assembly, though.

"It's a lot of fun," Carolina says. "Mr. Hernandez even lets us play some top forty songs now. We also got a lot more students to join this semester."

Mammonton Industries made sure the music program was safe for a long time, thanks to their very big donation. Mr. Barnett brought the check to Principal Li after his trip to Hawaii. At the assembly for the check presentation, Mr. Barnett looked tan and relaxed and didn't seem caffeinated at all. Mr. Mammonton never made an appearance, though, even when Principal Li invited him.

The factory is almost back to the way it was, but I read in the newspaper that Mammonton Industries was going to start a new line of products using eco-friendly materials. I'm sure they're still making stuff that's questionable, but hey, at least they're doing something the right way.

"Anybody take my place at triangle?" I ask.

"No," Carolina says. "Though if you ever want to come back, it will be right there waiting for you. It isn't exactly the most popular instrument."

"I don't know," I say. "I'm a little rusty. It might take me a while to get back into the swing of things."

Carolina stares at me for a moment.

"I can't tell if you're being serious or not," she says.

When I grin, she lets out a laugh. It sounds really nice.

"For an instrument that's pretty simple to operate, I managed to make it more complicated than it needed to be," I say. "But I'm excited to see your next concert."

"We'll all be happy to see you in the audience," Carolina says.

"Even Veronica?" We never really connected. She's okay, but I don't see us getting together and having pizza outside of a group hang.

"I know Mr. Hernandez will be," Carolina says. I know *that's* true. He made a bronze plaque in my honor that's hanging in the band room. It's engraved to read: WITH OUR GREATEST APPRECIATION TO LILA MORADI. THE MUSIC PLAYS ON BECAUSE OF HER AND HER DEVOTION TO THE ARTS AND HER FRIENDS.

"And I'll be happy to see a friend in the crowd," Carolina continues, but she sounds a little shy when she says it. I guess she's making sure that I *am* a friend. We never really declared it, but I figured inviting her to a concert would prove I am.

"Just to be clear, the friend you're talking about is me,

right?" I ask with a smile. She smiles back. There. Now it's decided. We are pals. We don't need a plaque to announce it either.

"Hey, excuse us," a kid in the row in front of us says. The kid's friends look excited and a little nervous. All of them are around our age. "Are you from the I Can't Believe It's Not Juice commercial? The one with all the WNBA players?"

The commercial has been airing for about two months now. It was really surreal being on a video shoot with some of my favorite players. It only lasted a few hours, but it was cool to take selfies with pro players and see my face on TV with theirs. I thought about Felise the whole time. The money I Can't Believe It's Not Juice gave me was put in a trust by my parents for my college tuition. Mr. Stuart at the Providential Hills Bank, the guy who wouldn't give me a loan, treated me a lot differently when I showed up with my parents and a check. Then he looked disappointed when we decided to go with Mrs. Banmeke as our financial advisor instead.

"Yeah, yeah, it's her," Parisa says. She rolls her eyes but lets a smile peek out too. She acts kind of annoyed that

I get attention like this, but I also think she's a little proud of me.

"Awesome! Would you mind taking a selfie with us?" another one of the kids in the group asks.

I'm still not used to getting attention from strangers. Sometimes I don't do what people ask, like when they want me to pose for a photo with them. I feel a little guilty when I say no, because I don't want to disappoint anybody, but I also remember that setting boundaries is okay. It's nothing a person should feel sorry about.

"I will if you tell me your names," I say to the group. "I'm Lila." The kids all introduce themselves. It turns out they go to a nearby school. Melanie plays their school in soccer and gets to talking with them when they realize they have friends in common. Their group takes a photo with our group, which feels a lot better than being in the photo by myself.

The lights start to dim as a voice booms out of the arena speaker system. The arena isn't even halfway full yet. People are still finding their seats, snacks in hand, settling down for the show to begin.

"Welcome to Pop Fest 3000," the announcer says. Carolina, Melanie, and I cheer, but the crowd isn't very loud. "Please give a warm hand for a brand-new artist making her stage debut today, Gwendolyn Jackson!"

"Oh, jeez, the opening act's got an opening act," Parisa says. "Can't be that good."

"Why don't we wait and see?" I say. Sometimes I check Parisa's negative attitude, like I imagine Felise would if she were here. "Maybe Gwendolyn is up-and-coming."

The band members walk onstage. A drummer, a bassist, a guitarist, and a singer I guess is Gwendolyn Jackson. She has long braids, beautiful dark skin like Carolina, and an awesome jean jacket with gemstones on it. She looks to be around Parisa's age.

"Well, I've never heard of her," Parisa says, folding her arms across her chest. I want to tell Parisa that she sounds like a know-it-all, but before I can, the band starts to play an upbeat R&B/pop hybrid.

"Hi, Providential Hills," Gwendolyn says into the microphone with a shaky voice. She pushes a braid behind her ear and looks nervously out at the crowd. "H-how are you all feeling tonight?"

There isn't much response. I let out a loud whoop—because I'm excited, but also because I know what it's like to have a lot of eyes on you, even in a small space, and how scary that can be. I can't imagine being a pop star performing in front of thousands.

Carolina, Melanie, and the friends we made in front of us follow my lead, shouting and cheering too.

The drummer kicks things off into high gear with an incredible solo. She looks so much like Gwendolyn, the two could be related. They could even be fraternal twins. I can't imagine Parisa and me playing in the same band. She'd tell me I was offbeat and we'd have to practice all the time.

"Hey, the drummer is pretty great," Melanie says, clapping in time. She's not the only one who thinks so. The crowd trickles in and is getting more and more hyped by the performance.

Gwendolyn Jackson looks over her shoulder at the drummer, who gives a nod. Then Gwendolyn turns back around and starts to sing into the microphone.

"Wow," Melanie says. Wow is right! Gwendolyn has a powerful and melodic voice like I've never heard before. She's so talented!

"Magnificent!" Carolina yells as the crowd grows louder. Even Parisa is clapping along. She doesn't have a critical word to say. When Gwendolyn finishes, she's met with roaring applause.

"Thank you so much!" Gwendolyn says into the mic, her head held a little higher and her shoulders more relaxed. "I never thought I'd be able to sing on a stage like this, but when an opportunity comes around, you have to take a chance." My arms prickle with goose bumps. "I wouldn't be here without the support of my band." Gwendolyn points to her guitarist and introduces him as Gus, who does a little ten-second solo. Then it's the bassist Mac's turn, also gracing us with an interlude.

"And last but not least," Gwendolyn says, waving her hand toward the drummer. "The unbelievable and always magical Felise!"

The drummer goes into a showstopping solo, and I'm not surprised in the least.

When she finishes, she throws a drumstick high in the air. The audience may not understand why or how, but it seems to float back down into her hand.

Felise winks at the crowd, but it feels like she's winking right at me.

Gwendolyn goes back to singing. As more people enter the arena, they're all entranced by her set, cheering when she hits a high note and dancing when she sings the chorus of a song that's sure to be a hit.

"What a superstar!" Parisa shouts in my ear. With Felise in Gwendolyn's corner, I have no doubt the whole world will know who she is soon enough. Fans will be humming her songs for decades to come.

"Lila? Are you okay?" I turn to my sister. She looks worried. "You're crying."

I didn't realize I was.

"I'm great," I say with a laugh, not bothering to wipe my eyes. I'm just so happy to see an old friend.

"Thank you so much, Providential Hills," Gwendolyn says before taking a bow. The musicians in her band keep playing when she goes backstage. The crowd chants for an encore, but I cheer for someone else.

"Yay, Felise!" I scream at the top of my lungs.

"Are you cheering for the drummer?" Parisa asks with a laugh. She ruffles my hair. "You're too funny."

When I cheer for the drummer a second time, Felise hears me. She may look a lot different, but I'd recognize the smile she gives me anywhere.

Gwendolyn comes back onstage to give the crowd what they want. She starts to sing another song, and everyone loves it.

But I keep watching my old friend doing what *she* loves to do: be a lucky star and help others shine just as brightly.

About the Author

Sara Farizan is the author of the middle-grade graphic novel *My Buddy, Killer Croc* from DC Comics, illustrated by Nicoletta Baldari. She is also the author of many young adult books that won awards and stuff. She likes cartoons, is Persian like Lila, and wishes she could win a shooting contest, but her jump shot is very rusty. She lives in Massachusetts. You can learn more about her and her books at www.sarafarizan.com.